MW01273488

# IN THE WORDS OF
# OLYMPIC PENINSULA AUTHORS
## *Volume 3*

Compiled and edited by Linda B. Myers and Heidi Hansen
Cover design and photo by Alan Halfhill
Interior design by Heidi Hansen

Published by H3 Press, PO Box 312, Carlsborg, WA 98324

ISBN: 978-0998252667

Acknowledgement is made for permission to publish:

# DEDICATION

To the adventures and solace our Peninsula provides

# CONTENTS

*Author Intro*

# DIANNE L. KNOX

Is it a poem yet? I ask this question, often. Unlike the expected nine-month gestation of my daughter, my poems are born with varying nurturing. Some are fully fleshed as soon as the words appear, requiring no incubation or staying in my body, my head. Others remain in a "gestative" state on scattered sheets, awaiting further coddling. Appearances are sometimes totally unlike original conception, unrecognizable, even to me. Life and poetry surprise.

I have been writing in my head, forever. My young-teen friend, Sue, and I wrote what we called "Mysties." Not so mysterious, really. But, fun. Sue has remained my friend, confidant, and laugh companion. If you find one like her, keep her. I am influenced so much by my relationships, often transparent in their effect on me, spilling onto my yellow pads. Loss has played into my words, hard, grieving loss. And, now, new-found love.

I find an increasing ability to communicate my poetry at open mics in the Pacific Northwest. I hear that I am successful in hiding my deep difficulty of speaking to a group. Nerves slim down and I reduce shaking to a minimum with familiar faces. I'm happy to be a part of the talented area writers. Read us, we will give you words to fill your soul.

Contact Dianne at dianneknox@icloud.com or ddiseth@q.com
She would love to hear your comments. Really.

## COPPER RIVER REDUX

Copper River Salmon
Is on its way again
But this season
My appetite has filled

I will no longer drool
Over the counter
Where we met
Longing for that look

It took several years
To realize this position
Waiting for the perfect meal
Which arrived

In a blue shirt
With blue eyes
An Austin Healy
And an English Springer Spaniel

I am curious
What the fourth installment
Of this saga holds
2020 looks promising.

# LURES

Foggy morning horns
Misty moist air
Halibut season in session

Burn-off mid-morn
Or mid-day
Predicts a small catch
Fish strut on the bottom
Chests out
Having escaped the lures

Their precise movements
Will show on the bottom feeder finder
On a cool clear morning
Another day
No horns
When a casual stroll
Brings an irresistible
Taste in the water
A hefty price per pound

The biggest not the tastiest
But the most intelligent
Having watched compatriots
Succumb to temptation
Ending up in freezers
Or on dining tables

Pay attention to warning sounds of life
So when you hear sirens
You may swim about in opaque waters
Postponing hooks and lures.

# MEDITATIVE WAYS

There must be meditation
In a riding lawn mower
A steady noisy way
Disturbing my quiet way

Woodworkers find way
In a low, slow sanding sound
Bakers in turning thump of a rolling pin
Harley bikers in thundering wheel spin

Gardeners dig and pull
Rhythm obvious at harvest
A painter's meditative strokes merge
In finished canvas

A house-painter's no-drip skill
Appears on dried clapboard
Fishermen find meditation
In gentle casting, waving line
Tempting fly too much for a fish to resist

And, yes, there is focus, a meditative way
Of a person with a weapon firing rounds
Perfecting aim
Finding target's middle

A musician says it loud and proud
Hips shake, a black Sly Stone
Motown's love-child voices discrimination
All while rocking meditation

A knitter's adept needles click
Calming yarn into a vibrant pattern's lick
A story-teller's voice relaxes
A listener's wandering ear

We find a meditative state
In life's repetitive verbal gait
In vision's spectrum we hear a new color
See a new sound taking us to a place before unfound

## NO!

He never said no to her
She never said no to him.
He always said yes to her
She always said yes to him.

They needed each-other's breath
Each-other's depth
Wanted each-other's warmth
Each-other's constant growth.

Accepted their limitations
Stood by during frustrations
Living their seasons
Loving the reasons

How does this consciousness happen
Two people
Hearing, respecting on a level
Not comprehended by others

She never said no to him
Until it was time to go
He never said no to her
But, yes, he had to go.

# APPLE

You cannot purchase
This fine fruit
Taste, you will never know
It fell from no tree

Truth, knowledge, wisdom
Are visions, inedible
Enlightenment plays with shadows
Layers of color calm you to your core

Lion face peaks through green hieroglyphics
Yellow woman with visible spine
Hides behind a yellow curtain
On the right side

Was I meant to find these subliminals
Or was it luck
After staring intently
For what seemed lengthy

Exact translation escapes me
Except connection
With Apple's creator
Tempting me to feel her truth. I know.

## PARTS

When your world falls apart
Your parts fall everywhere
Mess, clutter are all there
Everywhere each and everywhere
There
Parts, departing, departed
Split into a thousand splinters
Pricking your skin
Stabbing your life to death

If you can collect the pieces
Put them together
Assemble a semblance
Of a world
You've known
To move onto
Neatness restored
Ordered, transformed
Into a life
Containing those bits
That fit
You've made it.

# SLOW DANCE

Do you know how to slow dance
A dance that has meditation
Between steps
A dance that suspends time
Between heartbeats
Halts after you breathe in
Relaxes on the out

A dance so slow
Fingertips drip down a cheek's skin
Pause on each pore
Long enough to absorb heat
Feel soft fuzz
Then drift to the next beat

Do you know how to slow dance
Move muscles so slightly
Intently
The only discernible movement
Felt by your partner
Seen by no one.

Fanned hand
Presses your back
Leads you with light pulses
In rhythmic sway

Do you know how to slow dance
Melt into flow
Glide and slide
With no one else to know
How completely you have let go?

# WAILING WHALE

She carries her pup on her head
Letting go, she cannot
The possibility causes dread
Losing her life's connection
Her life's direction
Her purpose, her reproduction

Mating for life
Waiting for death
Whale wailing in grief
Her baby's large black and white Orca hearse
Herself

Carried in gestation
Now carried in frustration
How could this mother fail
In protecting from illness
Her precious cargo
Her baby whale?

She glides through water
Guarding her first-born, now still
From predators and others
Who might take her pup
Against her will

We know her pain, feel her anguish
With each mournful splash
See what our parallel future
Could extinguish

How much longer will she hold both up
Her spirit declining along with her pup
J35 teaches us our meaning
Caring for our habitat perpetuates life
The alternative, grieving.

# THIS MAN'S HEART

This man's heart
Is in his eyes
On my eyes
Beating away any gray

This man's hands
Are full of me
On me, in me
Around me

This man's love
Is pounding in my soul
Visible in his touch
Felt in every glance

This man's energy
Is captured in my skin
On my skin
I am so near him

This man
Sees me feels me
Comes close to me
Knows me

Each touch is the heart
I see in his eyes.

# BOOKS – KITA

Kita loves to read
He will race over to my tan chair
Look into my eyes until
I am sitting down
Wait for me to put a pillow
On my lap
Then a book on the pillow
Before he lies comfortably
Down by and on my feet
He will stay there until
His attention goes to a noise
Outside or a scratch he
Needs to take care of
Then lies down again
The phone rings he sits up
Leans against my leg
I resume reading
He lies down
We keep this up all afternoon
Late into the evening
Because
Kita loves to read.

# FALLING

At what point
Have you stopped falling
Are fully felled
No longer dizzy
With the height
Allowing your weight
To be carried
In another's heart

At what point
Do you stop questioning
Your serendipitous fortune
Of finding treasure
On your doorstep
Moments before
You were to give up the search
Settle into your private peace

At what point
Do you accept
That you are deserving
Of this fine felled future.

# GOODWILL

She tries on friends like clothes
Then, leaves them abandoned
In a Goodwill bin
Their sizes ill-fitted to her taste

They will find new homes
Appreciative bargain-hunters
Will see more wear in well-worn
Fabrics of life

Others will try on personalities
She has tossed aside
See with fresh eyes
Worth in differences
Value in disagreements
Wealth in divergent dialog

Cast-offs will find their way
Into hearts open to experience
Forgetting about being thrown
Into a heap of under-valued friendship

They come alive again
Appreciated anew
In relationships
Where they're not
Taken for granted

# THE WORST ART

The worst art
Is the art that's kept inside
That doesn't see daylight
That knows no criticism.

The worst art
Has not been born
Has not cried out
I'm here, cut the cord.

The worst art
Is hidden, not shared
Not spoken, not seen, not heard
Is left inside screaming to be let go.

The worst art
Is not written, not sung
Not laughed at
Not cried about.

The worst art
Won't be recognized or acclaimed
Its soul
Has not been released.

The worst art
Is begging to escape
To an audience
Willing to pay with its ears and eyes.

*Author Intro*

# HEIDI HANSEN

At an early age, I learned the power of words. Given an option, I will always chose an essay test over True/False. My footing in journalism side-stepped into marketing. After a career marketing high tech products and services, I became an entrepreneur, first operating a gift basket business in Silicon Valley, then as a Realtor in the Pacific Northwest. All along the way, writing was the common thread, weaving words to create an idea or portray a product.

Two books of my short stories have been published, *A Slice of Life* and *A Second Slice*. I co-founded Olympic Peninsula Authors in 2017, and edited their three volumes of anthologies, *In The Words Of Olympic Peninsula Authors*. I am also a member of Northwest Independent Writers Association (NIWA) and a contributor to their 2019 anthology.

In Sequim, WA, you may find me leading a spontaneous writing group at the library, and hosting a monthly open mic for writers. Representing Olympic Peninsula Authors, I enjoy booth duty at local farmer's markets and bazaars promoting and selling books by local authors.

My story, "The Last Time I Saw Billy" appeared in the July/August 2019 issue of *Writer's Digest* as the short story winner. Another of my short stories is included in the 2019 Peninsula College literary magazine, *Tidepools.*

Reach Heidi at heidi@olypen.com

# BOOMERANG

It wasn't because of a geography lesson but the distribution of a toy that I became aware of Australia. The boomerang was an obtusely-angled slice of wood which when thrown would spin back to the thrower. Totally dependable. Repeatable. It was awesome. It was distributed by Wham-O, the same people who brought us the Hula Hoop and the Frisbee. Advertised on television, I gazed in awe at its return to the thrower, over and over again. Did this really work? What were its magical powers? Could anyone learn to do it?

That Christmas my sister, Karen, unwrapped a brightly-wrapped box that held a Boomerang. It was the best present under the tree, though several were more expensive. Outside, my father scanned the instructions, then hurled the toy into the air. It flew across the driveway and far into the ten-acre orchard which was our backyard. We watched in amazement. It turned and came back, but fell short of returning to Dad's hand. Over and over, he practiced as we children stood begging at his feet. "Let me, let me." "It's mine, I got it from Santa." "I can do it, I know I can."

He had to take a step forward, hand outstretched, before it came to him. That's when he handed it to Karen.

She stepped up like she was going to bat, and with all her nine-year-old might, threw it as she had seen Dad demonstrate.

I should add that my dad is right-handed as are all of us. Karen is the lone lefty in our family. Her toss did not follow the same trajectory. If Dad's went left, hers went right and instead of turning and coming back, hers fell from the air and landed in the dirt. Far down the path into the orchard.

We raced out to retrieve it.

Dad yelled, "Throw it back towards me."

Karen looked at the toy, turning it over to see if there was a "this side up" instruction. She shrugged her shoulders and hurled it toward Dad. We waited, watching for the boomerang to turn and come back. Again, it went in a straight path, right into Dad's shins. He was hopping mad and retreated into the house.

"Let me try," I whined. She glowered at me but handed it over. I stood like Dad and tried in every way to repeat what I had seen him do. I tossed the boomerang and as I prayed for it to make the return flight, it did. Karen stomped her feet and tore it out of my hands. She dashed it to the ground and kicked it.

Two younger sisters picked it up and threw it about, not with the same care or precision. When Paula tried, the damn thing came right back to her. Karen had enough and grabbed it.

"It's mine," she said. With boomerang in hand, she tromped off into the middle of the orchard. "Leave me alone," she shouted back should anyone consider following her.

At dinner, Dad asked Karen if she had any luck in getting the boomerang to return.

She looked down, moving her food around on her plate, and said that she lost it.

After breakfast the next morning, we formed a search party. Weaving our way through the trees, eyes downcast, but sometimes looking upward into the branches, we did not find it.

In the Spring, the orchardist was busy. He needed to cultivate the ground and get ready for irrigation. In turning the soil, he spied the boomerang.

"Karen, Karen," he yelled as he jumped off the tractor in our driveway. "I found it."

In his hands, he clutched the boomerang.

Karen took it and scuffed her way around the back of the barn. Bad mood was written all over her, so we kept clear.

At dinner, Paula announced that John had found Karen's boomerang. Dad said, "Karen, we'll go have another practice after dinner."

Karen glowered, "I threw it and it went up on the barn roof."

Now there was a place none of us went.

But in the Summer, the cherry plum tree was full of fruit, small cherry-sized plums. When Grandmother visited, she made jam.

"Girls, climb up on that roof and get me some bucketfuls," she instructed.

It was easy to climb up on the abandoned chicken coop next to the barn. I put the ladder in place and went up, Paula and Darcy followed. Each with a bucket which we filled with only the best of the fruit. If it was squishy or the birds had got to it first, we left it or kicked it to the ground. With three full buckets, Granny would have plenty. I climbed down with one bucket then did it two more times. The younger girls were good pickers, but too small to handle the bucket and the ladder.

On seeing me come in, mom asked, "Did you clean off the roof?"

I shook my head.

"Take the broom and sweep it, no reason to leave all that up there to rot."

I dragged the broom and climbed the ladder one more time. I swept the roof, pushing the leaves, fruit and other debris down to the ground. Where the tree branches tangled in the roof of the barn, I saw the boomerang. That was the upside for having to pick the cherries and clean the roof. I couldn't wait to show Karen.

She took one look at it and dissolved into tears. I followed her as she raced up the stairs to the bedroom we shared.

"I hate that stupid thing," she cried.

"I'll help you," I said.

"No, I hate it. I buried it in the orchard…"

"And John found it."

"I threw it up on the roof where no one could find it…"

"And I found it."

She glared at me.

"I guess you can see that it does work. It keeps coming back to you."

## THE LETTER

I'm writing to explain about when my mother had a particularly bad day—a bad day by what she called her mom-o-meter. She would call us together and say, "We need to play a game.

"What game?" my brother Mike would ask.

"A TV game," she'd say. "A very special one."

By the time I was four, I knew exactly what was going to happen when she would call us to her after a bout of slamming doors or kitchen cabinets. In fact, because I was fifth of five, it was often my job to help "bring the treasure chest forth." It wasn't really a treasure chest, just a cardboard box with "Lucky Strike" on the side. Mike and Debby colored it with their crayons to make it resemble a pirate's chest. The box was kept in mom's closet, under the long dresses. We would carefully bring it to the living room, then everyone would take their places.

Mike being the oldest always got to play the part of Jack Bailey and mom was always the contestant. Tommy never wanted to play because he didn't have much of a part, being the second eldest boy.

In the box was a long red cape with a white fur collar, long white gloves, a gold crown with big red jewels, a bouquet of red plastic roses and an broken flashlight that had been altered to look like a microphone.

Lastly, all five kids would  go through a box of papers— colorful pictures we had cut out of magazines. These were to be the prizes. What five prizes would we pick today? We had to do this without consulting mom, and there would be rewards if we picked things she really wanted that day.

Debby would sit down at the piano and begin to bang out her version of "Pomp and Circumstance." Mike took the microphone and shouted "Who wants to be Queen for a day?" Then he exclaimed, "Because of her excellent mom skills and extraordinary cooking ability, the judges agreed that Mrs. Marjorie Probst was indeed Queen for the Day."

Mom would come center stage and "ooh" and "my gracious me" and then crouch down so that Liz and I could wrap the red cape over her shoulders. Tommy brought the crown to Jack Bailey to put on the Queen. Debby played another round on the piano. Then Mike said in his best Jack Bailey voice, "and Mrs. Marjorie Probst wins today. Ta da!" Each of us would present her with a cut-out advertisement for what we hoped she really wanted.

One time Mike gave her a matching washing machine and dryer. Debby always gave her the electric dishwasher because washing dishes was Debby's job. Tommy bowed down with a flourish and presented mom with "a brand new car." Liz gave mom a fur coat, even though we lived in Arkansas and nobody wore fur coats. I always gave her the same thing, the one thing I wanted more than anything else in the world, a puppy.

"Thank you, thank you, thank you," she would say.

Then we would wait. What would she do next?

One time she sat there for a whole hour with a smile on her face. Another time she tossed down the red roses and said, "Okay, back to work." We liked it when she said, "That was fun, let's all go out for ice cream."

\* \* \*

"Are you kidding me? You can't write about that. Not the Queen for a Day thing. Write about something else," Debby said reading over my shoulder.

"Why do you say that? It was a special time."

"Yeah, special like it shows how crazy she really was."

"I think it shows how important it was to her."

"And another thing, that wasn't fur on the red cape."

"It wasn't, what was it?"

"First off, the cape was an old bedsheet and the fur collar was three maxi pads taped to the sheet."

"But it looked like fur. Mom called it ermine."

"It was white with some black lines and circles drawn on it. I guess you might want to believe it. You were pretty young back then."

"When was the last time we played it?"

"You don't remember?"

"No."

"It was when Mike was in high school, and mom wanted to "play TV" when he had friends over. He protested and she said, "The more the better—more prizes." Mike said, "No," real loud and scary. Mom started screaming. It wasn't long after that that she went away, and Aunt Erma came to live with us."

"Yeah, Aunt Erma. She didn't want to "play TV" or anything. She was tough."

"She called it tough love."

"And then Mike went off to college, you got married and I came to live with you. It was better than with Aunt Erma."

"Yeah, but Tommy and Liz were stuck there with her till they got out of school. I think that's why Liz got pregnant. Anything to get out of that house."

"Then mom came home."

"And oh my god did she throw a fit when she found out Queen for a Day was cancelled the week before she came home. If you listened to her, it was all she lived for."

"She used to come to my school and try to get me to go home to play TV with her. It was kind of sad, kind of spooky."

"You never went did you?"

"No, I said I had to go back to class. I was sad because she was my mom..."

"Yeah, we all have that torn feeling between wanting to be the good kid to our mother and realizing that she was crazy as a loon. We have to watch out for ourselves. When was the last time you saw her?"

"It was before she went to Vegas."

"That was a pretty spectacular episode."

"Who knew she would do that?"

"I know. Jack Bailey got a restraining order against her and she got arrested. First there in Vegas, then again when she showed up at his house in Beverly Hills."

"She just wanted to be Queen for a Day."

"Look where that got her. Now her lawyer wants us to write letters to the court asking for leniency. I don't know what to say other than that she needs help. Mom asked me what happened to the treasure chest. I'm worried she wants to wear the cape and crown to court."

"So you don't think writing about how important that show was to her will help explain her obsession with Jack Bailey?"

"Hmmm when you put it that way, it was always being played out while we were growing up. Maybe it is the right thing to write about. Go ahead, finish the letter."

\* \* \*

So Judge, please understand that for the eight years that the television show was on, it saved my mother's sanity—it gave her something to look forward to, some way out of the life she had, though there was no way she could make it from our backwoods little town in Arkansas to Los Angeles to be a contestant. At sixteen, she had a child, then another, and another and another till she had all five of us. None of her husbands stayed long enough to form a bond with his child. Until she married a man named Sam Jones. He was my father. He loved us all and was a good man but he was struck down by a big semi that ran off the highway to avoid a dog. The driver lost control and plowed right through the hardware store where daddy worked. That's when mom started losing touch with reality. She just wanted one chance to be Queen for a Day. We could have used any of the prizes they gave away on that show, any one of them would have made our life better.

So you see, when she got things straightened out and they let her come home from the mental hospital, it broke her that Queen for a Day had been cancelled. When Tommy graduated, they played Pomp and Circumstance and that blew her away because that was the Queen for a Day music. She left after that on her quest to talk Jack Bailey into one more show. Just for her.

Sincerely,

Ms. Jackee Bailey Jones

# THE STRUGGLE

Violet McKinsey leaned back in her seat and took her husband's hand as the train left the station. Violet was struggling with right and wrong. She knew the difference, but she'd done wrong.

"It'll be a great vacation," Henry said, squeezing her hand.

"I love you Henry," she said.

The train passed through familiar neighborhoods. It would take another half hour of frequent stops before it would get up to speed. Violet closed her eyes and wished this to be the beginning of happiness. She heard a familiar sound, the slight flap of Henry's lips as he exhaled. A sure signal he was asleep. They had been married for thirty years. She wondered what secrets they kept from each other. She knew what she held secret.

She hadn't intended the affair. It started with a simple flirtation in a ceramics class. She wanted to learn to throw a pot on a wheel. Jack was the other older student and together they laughed at their lopsided creations while the younger students seemed to be artisans. Laughing led to coffee, then one of them opened the door sharing some inner truth. That is what she missed with Henry. She didn't know what was going on with his work or among his closest friends. Everything between them felt on the surface, not deep-rooted like it had been. And then, she knew what Jack was thinking, what was going on his life. He knew what she was thinking, what she needed, wanted, and he kept saying and doing those things that made her smile. It was easy to touch him, let him touch her. Suddenly they were planning weekend escapes. Henry hardly noticed. He didn't question her plan to visit the wine country with an imaginary girlfriend, or a shopping trip to New York. He didn't ask about what she bought, and did she see a show. He kissed her goodbye and hello and life went on.

Henry stirred in his sleep and grumbled as if reacting to her thoughts. She tried to think quieter. She still held his hand, he squeezed it now and then, and settled back into a soft snore. The last thing she wanted was to hurt Henry or to end their marriage. She marveled at the idiocy of her thought. She had a love affair with another man but didn't want to end her marriage or hurt her husband. What had she wanted? Some attention? To be in the spotlight one more time before she admitted she was old? Perhaps she told herself. Perhaps that was all it was. Selfish me.

She dropped Henry's hand, wrapping her arms around herself not in an embrace of love, but in disgust and fear. She would still be playing around with Jack if not for the demands he began to make. How long did it take before he wanted more than she was willing to give? When they were in Napa, it was perfect. When they were in New York it began to be less perfect. First, she caught him going through her purse. Then she found him taking photos of her while she slept.

"What? What are you doing?"

"Not to worry, they're just for me. I love you so much."

As he said this, she felt a chill. She tried to forget it in their lovemaking, but there was a bubble of doubt floating around inside. As her concerns multiplied, she faced reality. Why was Jack so enamored with her? She was a married, middle-aged woman with no future for them. Why was this enough for him? What kind of a monster was she? If not a monster, surely a fool.

One night when Henry walked in their front door, the phone rang. She answered it.

"Did I catch you at a bad time?" Jack whispered on the other end.

"Can't talk now." She said and hung up.

"What's for dinner tonight? Wanna' go out?" Henry said.

"I've got dinner in the oven, chicken pot pie." She said, then turned away and replayed the phone call. Jack never called on her house phone, they always used their cell phones. She was careful to remove his voicemails and delete the history should Henry look at her phone, but he did not. Why had Jack whispered like that? Why would he start with "Did I catch you at a bad time," as if he knew that Henry just walked in? Was he watching the house? She picked up the phone and checked the caller id. It was his cell phone number. He could be sitting outside now.

All this made her heart ache and her nerves raw. She hated herself for what she had done. She was unfaithful to Henry and had violated her own values. *I have whored myself for a little attention* she thought. She turned and looked at Henry as he slept. Did he know? Did he have any idea? Would Jack contact him and tell him, show him the photos, make him realize what had been going on? If he did, how would Henry react?

She closed her eyes as if to stop this painful introspection. I need to put this behind me. Will Jack let me go quietly?

She called it quits shortly after that phone call. Just as their relationship began when they developed trust, it was over when that trust was broken. He cried and said that he hadn't meant to call her at her home, but she wasn't answering her cell phone. She pulled out her cell phone, buried in her purse, and there were two calls. She could never be sure if they came just before the phone rang in the house or just after she hung up.

He followed her the next week when she went out, so he was watching her. He would show up sauntering down the aisle in the grocery store. "Oh, hi Violet. Long time no see."

"Imagine seeing you here." He said when she went to the pottery shop to pick up her last project. He was there, but he had no pieces to fire or pick up. He was just there.

The last time she saw Jack was when she went to meet Henry at his office. Walking into the lobby, she saw Jack standing at the reception desk, staring at her. That was the last straw. She told him he was not to contact her again or to follow her.

"Don't make me get a restraining order, Jack." She said.

"Or what? You're going to huff and puff and blow me away?" He laughed at her.

Then she did what she should have done in the beginning. She went online and googled him. There were numerous reports from women claiming he stalked them, that they got restraining orders which he disobeyed.

Henry said, "Honey, you seem a little tense, Anything bothering you?"

"Perhaps a week away in the country." She said.

"That's a good idea." She thought he meant for her to go alone or with a girlfriend, but then he added, "Let's go next week. I could use a break too."

She fell back in love with him. There was nothing being held back but the ugly affair and she was pedaling as fast as she could to put it behind her.

Henry stirred again and awoke.

"Guess I needed that nap. Now I need the bathroom." He rose and ambled down the car.

Violet exhaled trying to relieve the tension. She really wanted to enjoy the trip. A hand touched her shoulder, and she jumped. She turned assuming it was Henry only to find Jack leering at her.

"What? What are you doing here?" she sputtered.

"I'm missing you sweetie," he said with a grin. "Follow me up to the next car."

"No. We're through. Go." She said.

"We're in love." He said. "C'mon, we've got time for a quickie."

She wondered if the couple in front of her heard him. Henry would be back shortly. She steeled herself not to turn and look over her shoulder. She looked down at her feet; she would not look at Jack.

"Have it your way. You'll regret it," he said, then moved to the forward car.

After lunch, she fell asleep with her head on Henry's shoulder. He was reading a digital book and the rhythm of the train quickly put her to sleep. When she awoke, Henry was snoring, and it was dark outside. She thought they must be nearing their destination and looked around. Jack stood at the car entrance staring at her. She wondered if his stare had awakened her. She glared at him. He opened the car door and stepped onto the platform. She followed. He walked through the next car and onto the platform. She stopped there to confront him. He grabbed her shoulders and shook her, then pulled her close, holding her firmly.

"You're not going to do this to me," he snarled.

"It's over Jack. Let me go."

"I'm not going to do that. You can't get rid of me."

"Stop. Let go." She struggled to get out of his grasp. She could wiggle free from one hand but not both. She put her foot behind his trying to trip him. He pushed her against the railing between the cars. She fell to her knees. Through the grating she could see the tracks below. She felt the rush of air on her face as she stood.

"Stop fighting me! If you won't leave him, then you'll have to…"

Violet raised her knee and struck him in the groin. He doubled over in pain. And in that second, she backed out of his grasp. She looked into the car ahead and saw no one looking back. She turned her head to look into the car behind for help, but Jack propelled himself toward her, arms outstretched to grab her.

"You bitch! Just like all the bitches."

She jumped across the platform away from him as he fell on the spot where she had stood. He lunged toward her again but lost his footing and fell forward off the platform into the night.

There was a sound like "Oooff." Then there was only the sound of the train on the track. Violet stood looking into the night, wondering what to do. She stepped back into the car and into the restroom. She splashed cold water on her face, washed her hands and stared at her blank eyes in the mirror. She weighed the question of reporting a man overboard or not. Realizing it might be too late, she walked back through the car and took her seat.

Henry was still asleep. She nestled against him, her head resting on his shoulder.

As the train slowed coming into the station, Henry said, "Violet, wake up, we're here."

# DESTINATION

Marjorie and William Sterling boarded the cruise ship via wheelchairs. While both could walk, this saved a lot of time and stress, and alleviated falls. They were taken immediately to their stateroom, one with a wide balcony overlooking the San Francisco Bay. William breathed a sigh and said, "This is the way to go, first class."

"Indeed," Marjorie said, unpacking a carry-on.

"The view is splendid, better than I would have thought."

The steward hovered. "Is there anything I can bring you now? We'll leave the harbor in two hours. Dinner will be served at seven. Would you like to dine in your room tonight?"

"Is that offered?" Marjorie asked.

"Of course. We make every effort on these senior cruises to make your journey as pleasant as possible. You can fill out the menu on the in-room computer."

Marjorie looked at William and he nodded, "Yes, we'll dine in tonight. Thank you."

The steward bowed and opened the door to exit. Then he turned, "I almost forgot, there is celebratory champagne in your refrigerator. Would you like me to open and pour for you before I leave?"

"Oh, that would be fabulous," Marjorie said.

He deftly uncorked the bottle and poured two flutes, then set the bottle in the ice bucket before leaving the room.

Marjorie made her way to the veranda and sat down. "This is the life."

"It is my dear," William said taking the seat beside her.

"Here's to fifty-three years together." They clinked their glasses and sipped the champagne.

"And to what lies beyond," William said.

"Enjoyed all of it because of you," Marjorie said, patting William's hand.

"Everything settled then?"

"It is. Customer Relations will mail the letter to Holly."

On Friday, Holly received a letter from her parents. She turned the envelope over in her hand. It was unusual for her mother to write; she usually called. Holly wondered when she last spoke with her parents. Her life was busy with work and family. She felt guilty because her parents were alone across the country and her father's health was waning.

She tucked the envelope into her pocket, planning to read it during her son's soccer game later. Only rain cancelled the game, and she picked up pizza for the family that night.

Saturday her cell phone rang.

"Yes?" She said into the phone.

"Is this Holly Warburton?"

"It is," she said warily, assuming the caller was a solicitor, ready to disconnect to avoid hearing an offer.

"This is Micah McLaren and I am calling regarding Marjorie and William Sterling."

"Yes?" Holly said.

"Sorry to call with bad news…"

"Bad news? What bad news? Who is this?"

"Micah McLaren with the Valkyrie Cruise Line…"

"My parents? What cruise?" She stopped where she stood in the grocery store. "What? You must be wrong. My parents are at home…"

"Did you receive a letter from them yesterday?"

"I did…" *But I never opened it. Is it still in my jacket pocket? How would this person know that they sent me a letter? Is this a scam?*

"I am sure this is a shock, but I need to advise you that while at sea, Marjorie and William Sterling peacefully went in their sleep. As this occurred in international waters and per their request, their bodies were buried at sea…"

"What?" Holly plopped down in the cereal aisle. The colorful boxes lining the shelves faded into the background. "They're dead?" she said focusing on Tony the Tiger.

"Yes, sorry to have to advise you this way, but this is as they requested."

"What do you mean as they requested? Surely they did not know they would die in their sleep. What are you saying?" People stopped in the aisle, offering assistance. Holly waved them off.

His voice changed. He spoke deliberately as if he was accustomed to speaking with hysterical women. "Then you have not read their letter? You did not know that they were taking this cruise?"

"No. What cruise are you talking about?"

"It is the Valkyrie Cruise Line, we offer premium senior cruises…"

"My father was terminally ill. I can't see why they were taking a cruise at this time. My mother was in perfect health." Holly sobbed. *Could this be true?* She found herself asking Snap, Crackle, and Pop. The man on the oatmeal box gazed back kindly.

"You need to read the letter."

"Okay, okay. I have to go home to get it. I'm at the grocery store…"

"Go home. Read the letter. Call me if you need more information."

Holly rushed out of the grocery store, leaving her half-full cart in the cereal aisle. Her phone still in her hand, she dialed her mother's number. It rang and rang, then a message that the number was no longer in use. *What the hell?* She dialed their landline. Again, it rang and rang and then the message, "This number has been disconnected."

At home she stormed into the house and searched through the coats hanging in the hall closet. *Which one did I wear yesterday? What can the letter say that will explain this?*

Her husband, Roger, called to the kids, "Let's help mom with the groceries." They were out the door before Holly realized what they were doing and then back as quickly.

"Honey? Where are the groceries? I thought you went shopping?" Roger asked.

"Uh huh, I did, but…Here it is." Holly pulled the envelope from the pocket.

"What, what happened?"

"Oh, the damn letter." The envelope, a number ten, like a business mailing, was in her mother's handwriting. Holly tore it open and sunk down on the arm of a chair.

"What's that?" Roger asked with concern.

Holly waved her hand at her husband. She read, then her breath caught, and she let out a sob.

"What is it?" He moved across the room to read over her shoulder. "Who's taking a cruise? Who is this from?"

"It's from my mom. She and dad went on a cruise..."

"I thought he was in hospice..."

"He was..." Holly dissolved into her husband's embrace, sobbing. "They're dead."

"What? Who is dead? Your father?"

"My parents. They died at sea ..."

He let go a long string of questions but Holly was unable to acknowledge or answer. The kids stood in the doorway watching their parents, afraid to ask any questions. Finally, Roger took the hand-written letter from Holly and read it through.

> *Dear Holly,*
>
> *Your father is dying and the pain is intolerable. The doctors said there is nothing more they can do, but to try and keep him comfortable. I could not stand by and watch, and there is nothing more I could do to ease his journey. We have watched many of our friends suffer. It's horrible for the dying partner, often worse for the one left behind.*
>
> *When we learned about this cruise, it seemed the perfect solution. We will exit together and in a beautiful surrounding. We'll leave no funeral expense or arrangements to burden you. Our will leaves all our assets to you, and we are proud to say that we leave no debts. You have been the daughter we always wanted, and we will miss you but hope that we may reunite with you in the hereafter (if there is one).*
>
> *With love,*
> *Mother and Father*

Roger bent and picked up the envelope from the floor. Inside was a glossy color brochure, a cruise ship on the cover advertising "Your Final Destination" offered by the Valkyrie Cruise Line. It touted that patrons could embark at any port of call and select their departure date within the one-week sailing time. During their stay on board, they would have access to all the luxuries and services. A list of options under "Remains" allowed the passengers to choose between having their bodies returned to shore or buried at sea. A shaky hand had circled the latter. And under "Accommodations," there was another circle for the veranda suite. Roger cursed when he read the next section. Under "Demise," the choices included "Dinner and a Movie," "Injection," and "Drug of Choice." He hurriedly closed the brochure before Holly could read the circled selection.

Holly and her husband visited the local travel agency and learned that this final destination cruise is one of many services offered to seniors. Ships leave filled to capacity every Saturday and return empty the following Saturday. "And that is just here in our port," the woman behind the desk said. "They have many ports of call."

Information on the service was readily available. Hospice caretakers knew about it and suggested it to their patients. For some there was free passage when they could not afford it. "Not as many of the luxuries nor the veranda suite for those," one man said, "but it is a better way to go than expiring in a lonely hospital ward and being buried without a grave marker. Isn't it?"

At last Holly went to check their home. It was apparent they had no plans of returning. On the kitchen table was an official-looking envelope marked "Final Instructions." Inside were details about bank accounts, insurance policies and the deed to the house. Closets and cupboards had been cleared out. The refrigerator stood empty. Marjorie left some things – perhaps more to make Holly feel that she was gone for good. These things had been dear to Marjorie, pictures of family and close friends, her favorite books.

At the memorial service Holly said, "My parents chose to obey their marriage vow till death do us part, and even in death they went together."

*Author Intro*

# KIRSTI LEE

I was born and raised in West Seattle, to a large family of outdoors people. My father was a lumberman/ fisherman who retired from the Carlsborg Mill in the early 1960s.

We spent many days on the Olympic Peninsula, in the Straits and on the San Juan Islands as children. The Salish Sea was our playground.

When I retired from property management, I returned home to Washington, March of 2017 from Chicago-land.

Sequim felt like home the moment I arrived. The beauty of the Olympic Peninsula, has not lost its shine from my childhood.

I have had, since childhood, a deep and loving respect for nature and its creatures. My connection to these creatures is not a gift, it is who I am.

I am so grateful for the opportunity to share with others my love and the joy I receive each day living on the Olympic Peninsula, via the Olympic Peninsula Authors.

Contact Kirsti at kirsti54@yahoo.com

# THE DEATH OF AUTUMN

Slowly trickling blues and silver
waters sweet and cool.
Softly ticking moments gather
deep within their pools.

They change to roaring rivers
pounding banks as if in pain.
They fill themselves to bursting
with the coming of the rain.

Fading greens to gold and grey
yellows turn to dust.
The scent of autumn's shortening days
disappears and smells of must.

Hording birdsong in my heart
clinging to my youth.
I refuse the marching beat of time
and disavow the truth.

My flowers gone, my body slows
as sleep becomes more dear.
Autumn fades, the birds fly south
knowing winter's near.

The somber quiet of cooler days
when autumn breezes blow
makes autumn's death as cold and hard
as ice and freezing snow.

Change has come within myself
as well as on my Earth.
My tired soul has reached its end
seeking slumber's berth.

Awakened then to wind and rattle
and leaves begin to blow.
My love of fall and all its shades
makes it hard to let life go.

The resting time before the storm
is gone as nature has her way.
There's no stopping Northwest wintertime
as leaden clouds obscure the day.

I will surely miss the autumn sun
in death's deep, quiet field.
Winter ends, the seasons change
with loveliness its yield.

*Author Intro*

# JUDITH R. DUNCAN

I write about my chickens, dog, friends, and the beauty of the Pacific Northwest. My poems and prose are published in *Tidepools, Four Corners, Cirque, Ekphrastic,* and several local anthologies.

Judy can be reached at Judy1ster@gmail.com

## SAFE HAVEN

Flattery Rocks
to Kalaloch shore
sea urchins, sea stacks
surf, sand, spruce
salmonberry, salal
sword ferns
sea lions, sea otters
sockeye salmon
starfish, steelhead, shellfish
sanderling, skimmer
sandpiper, sandcastle
setting sun

# WINTER OF 2019

we don't get much snow
if we do
it only lasts a few

when we do
as this year, 2019
it's up to a big dog's nose

when we do
I love the inches, feet
spouse hates it

I play with dog
jumping in snow
up to big dog's nose

spouse grouses
starts blowing snow
up & down the road

snow life
is no life for
snow blowing spouse

# THIS IS YOUR LIFE

This is a Pass or Fail exam.
Complete it by 85 years, sooner
if health conditions require.

Consider each response an opportunity
to enhance your wealth, desire
or be a miserable failure.

Do not hesitate, time is running out.
Erasures & mark-overs are forbidden
get it right the first try.

The test concludes
with a dark tunnel, bright light.
Sorry if you don't see the light.

Good luck.

# THREE HAIKU

blubbered sea lions
sleep on rocky headlands
salmon swim safely


winter wind
uproots spruce
roiling surf


the sign reports
*Beach Logs Kill*
walking the beach

# WORD NERDS

Jane stomps down the stairs, tosses her gray hair out of her eyes and blocks a young woman carrying a toddler. "Don't go in there, they'll toss you out." The woman clutches her child and moves around the wild-haired elderly woman. Jane yells at the woman's back, "First time I've been kicked out of a restaurant."

Doris trails about five feet behind her friend. She is never comfortable with Jane's temper. Catching up she offers, "Why don't you come over, we'll sit on the patio, have a cup of tea."

Jane pats her hair in place and ignores the invitation. "Were we loud? Vulgar? The cashier claimed we were disturbing customers, running off business."

Doris tries again, "Come to my house. Calm down before you drive back to Sequim."

Jane cannot stop. "Do you think it was our discussion about constipated verbs, run-on sentences, or verbing nouns? Perhaps the last line of your haiku "husband snoring" versus "husband snores." Her voice becomes louder. She shakes her fist. "The old noun-gerund and noun-verb discussion boils my blood."

Doris jumps back from the shaking fist. "Then, I brought up the case of the past participle. You slammed your phone on the table when you didn't agree with Google."

Smiling, Jane says, "I knocked over my water glass."

"You splashed water all over the man behind you. How did you manage that?"

Jane heads for her car, then turns back to Doris. "Forget tea. Guess I'm banned from Toga's for life. Stinking gerunds, rotten abysmal gerunds–I said gerunds. How did I know the cook's name was Gerald?"

# GATHERING EGGS

This country is going to hell
in a hand-woven willow basket
trimmed in rough cedar
a loosely woven carrier of bitter words.

It carries our country's divisions–
politics red to blue
gender, racial collision
true, untrue.

Reaching under my hens
I gather eggs
listen to soft clucks
a momentary peace.

*published in Cirque, Vol. 10, No.1*

*Author Intro*

# ABIGAIL JONES

I am twelve years old and in the seventh grade. The subjects I look forward to studying are Science and English. In my free time I sew for my business, Abz and Eva Creations, and in the summer we sell at the Sequim Farmer's Market. I also love writing short stories and poems. I spend time studying medical terminology and biology. When I graduate high school, I want to study biology, chemistry, physiology, cell biology, and neuroscience. I plan on becoming a neuroscientist.

I wrote these poems to express my love for nature and how much beauty we can see around us if we just stop for a minute to look and listen. My favorite part about where I live is the mountains. They are such a striking picture of majesty and greatness, but when you walk through their forests you find peace and tranquility.

This year I was the chapter winner of The National Society of the Daughters of the American Revolution: American History Essay Contest. I have previously published two poems in the book *In the Words of Olympic Peninsula Authors Volume 2*.

# SONG OF THE EARTH

I hear the whispers in the willows
And the rustles of the trees.
A sparrow makes its nest
As it rustles through the leaves.
The spring breeze blows through the brush,
Feeling warm and mild.
The flowers poke their heads through
Looking like sunshine's child.
The wild grass sways in sync to the wind,
The saplings, they shake
And the bushes join in.
Rustling and howling
Brushing and buzzing at my feet.
I would do anything to go on a walk in spring,
Just to hear Mother Nature sing.

# BEAUTY OF THE NIGHT

The earth bulges up
To form mountainous peaks
And the valleys bow down
To their majesty

Waves crash down
On a glassy sea
And the wind whistles
A sweet melody

The trees and the plants
Stop to listen
to the lovely song
And to see the moon glisten

As they reach up their branches
To a star spangled sky
Colored with deep and dark
Shades of blue

Oh the beauty
Of the comets flying by
That even the mountains
Are inferior to

# STEPHEN WORKMAN

Born in Seattle during Arthur Langlie's second term as Washington State governor, I moved to the Olympic Peninsula in 2008.

A long time Husky fan, I received a Bachelor of Science in Building and Construction Management from the University of Washington in 1979. Then I built stuff for thirty years.

My current interests include advocating for better behavioral health patent care in America, awareness of stigma, and, writing.

I live in Port Angeles with my live-in ex-girlfriend, dog and cat. We dance the cha-cha to country songs on Thursday night at the Casino in Blyn.

Contact Stephen at workie@gmail.com

# THE SALISH SCENE

My Granny? She's got bullets in her head. There's more ammo in the rest of her, too. I overheard some guy on a whale-watching boat talking about a PBS Nova show he'd seen on Netflix. It was another JFK assassination conspiracy documentary. First, they showed a bullet shot into wood, to represent how deep a bullet might go. Then they shot a bullet into a giant sausage full of Jell-O'y stuff. Supposedly, the Jell-O stops a round cold, then a lab tech can take the slug and match it against other gun scratches on file. The lady he was hitting on said *Maybe I saw that show*, then barfed over the rail. The swells weren't bad, so maybe the lady's mom made her eat Jell-O against her will when she was a kid—some people react strongly to a bad memory like that. Who knows, they stopped talking after the puking. Anyway, the bullets in my Granny stay where they stopped, never analyzed, never matched to nothing. Granny's blubber stopped her bullets.

Come to think of it, us whales kinda look like giant sausages. My Granny's greasy fat halted the .45s, .223s, and various calibers plinked at her. Shotgun pellets, too, probably. Granny's blubber kept that ammo from hurting her organs, inside down farther. Since lead can't rust, those bullets lay still, below the dermis, with zero affect on her vitals. Some of those rounds in Granny must be, what...thirty, fifty, eighty-years-old? These days Granny can't remember all the times she got peppered...she is a hundred and two. Granny likes it when I tease her about being all shot up. *I'm packing lead*, she says. Our matriarch, she could care less. *I got thick skin*. Yah, riddled with bullets.

Granny's skin is thick. Old and scarred and all beat up. Over the years, she's crashed her body into all kinds of things. Drifting Japanese tsunami docks. Mastless capsized trawlers. Prominences on rocky headlands. *Granny, you need glasses, or what?* She's got all sorts of gashes, divots and disfigurements, pockmarks, scab-overs, hinky wounds. To hear her tell it, during the Truman administration she even had a long-line of halibut hooks trailing out her blowhole. Don't even mention the Navy's sound navigation and range testing. 235 decibels? *Dumbbells* in charge of that testing, but hey, that's just one fish's opinion. Granny's hearing was wrecked by those ultra frequencies for a couple years in the '70s. She went deaf and couldn't ping worth a damn. Bled out her eyeballs. Her audio and sonar reappeared finally, the bleeding stopped, but the pack still made her swim the perimeter. They'd lost trust in her leadership 'cause Granny kept bumping into the relatives, knocking them off course...even after her senses worked again.

Speaking of being off course, I got a cousin, Rodney, who can't stop diving the sewer pipe in the Strait. In fact, somebody asked me about Rodney just yesterday. *Oh he's down taking the pipe,* I guessed, 'cause that's where he usually is. Granny says Vancouver Island's been pumping their crap into the Strait since, well, she says *Since forever.* I reminded her that I dump in the Strait, too, and we got about eighty or so in our pod doing it willy-nilly...*Just saying, Granny.* But she insists Greater Victoria has thousands of thousands of people sending their scat down the chute, so maybe it is different. Rodney told me they screen out condoms and tampons—which is a good thing.

I'll be the first to admit, Rodney's a full-on weirdo. Very strange my cousin hanging around a sewer pipe all the time.

My other cousin, Bertie, who's also my aunt and my sister from my mom's side—trust me when I say whales' family trees are different than yours—is sure Rodney's huffing the pipe. Bertie's a girl, smaller than me, but she's got brains in a big way. She knows a lot and is crackerjack in the smarts department. Bertie's already learned every one of the pod's sagas, all the way back to the beginning. Damn amazing memory of hers! Tell her something, *Bam!*, it's locked in that giant noggin. When she's older, she'll be our priestess for sure, nobody touches that brainiac. So if Bertie says Rodney's huffing poo, I'm going with that.

Bertie explained it saying Canadians use lots of drugs. During the gray winters they take all kinds of antidepressants to lighten their moods. What happens is, a Victoria-ite gets a new pill prescription for say, Xanax, and flushes the expired pills out the pipe. Pills are too small to get screened, plus, they must be already dissolved, right? Bertie says Rodney's got a jones for the schedule four cures that spew out that cement vent. It's very low dose, so Rodney has to stay down there a while. *Anybody seen Rodney?* Granny says, *Rodney's not blessed upstairs.* No doubt and sucking down pill laden poo ain't gonna help that mush-mind any. When Rodney surfaces after sucking the pipe? It's not just the smell that clues us in to where he's been.

Last March we got Rodney away from the drain for an afternoon. Some people call us Southern Residents, and every March we honor some of our Southern Resident ancestors. That's not what we call ourselves, by the way. With Granny leading the pack, we headed south to the very end of Puget Sound for the remembering of the Olympia Six. Forty years ago, down where the Sound bottoms out, six of my relatives were chased by boats and planes, then netted off Athens Beach. Apparently it wasn't the first time our kin were corralled up and readied for sale to SeaWorld. This all went down way before my time, but for Granny, a forty-year-old memory? Still fresh. She was part of the larger group from which the eventual captives were split off and she witnessed it all. Granny really livened up telling it again; the separated members of the clan was chased around till exhausted, never gave up, got boxed-in, were harassed and finally lassoed. Local citizen provocateurs had seen enough sea mammal torture of this sort, so they protested the enslavement, and laws were changed to end the subjection. After a couple weeks all six whales either escaped or were released and the political mop-up from the Budd's Inlet Incident marked the end of whale abductions in Washington State. Rumor is the slavers moved on to waters where slaving remains legal. *That can't be true, can it?* Granny says captured whales were worth a hundred grand back then. Bertie says that would be a half-million today...I wonder what I'd do to get all I wanted?

On the way back from Olympia we dove past a sunken Desoto off Goose Point. Somebody'd rolled it off a dock after shooting the driver just above the left eye. Back then autos swooped and had lines with sweeping tails and fins—nice, cars modeled after beautiful creatures. The current moves good off Goose Point so that wreck ended up deep. Desoto 'Adventurer'—now there's a cool name for ya—it settled upright on the gravelly bottom with a busted antenna and trunk lid open. Now greenish and barnacled, the whitewalls on her still kinda glow. Whoever ditched it figured it wouldn't ever be found, and, except for us and the other fishes, it probably hasn't. The skeleton sits in the driver seat, hands still cuffed to the wheel. A little red octopus lives in the shot-up skull. While I imagined the crime, the car's front grill smiled at me like Granny does when she's asleep with her mouth open. Swimming past I wondered where the bullet ended up.

Most Thursdays me and Rodney look for trouble. We'll set free a buoy or chew through some shrimp-pot lines, you know, stuff like that. But last Thursday we got after some seals down by Nip George Bay for a change of pace. A rookery is there and Rodney, glassy-eyed, had a hankering for the wee seal. The backside of Leland Island has a long gravel stretch where pinnipeds sun while their mamas go fishing. *Well, lick my lips.* We cruised the strand with one eye out of the water till we spotted some tiny loungers. If you spook a couple a pups? Get them scampered into the water? *Yum and double-yum.* But we weren't more than a couple minutes into it when Rodney spied Mrs. Hoober on her cabin deck with a long gun up—taking aim. Rodney shouted *Dive, cousin, dive!* and we submerged quick, vamoosing outta there.

Swimming tandem down twenty feet, the bullets squirreled and fizzled to a foamy end above us. Out of range and along the bottom, we angled down the drop-off and glided low for ten minutes or so. We practiced slow rolls then surfaced near Goat Bluff. Rodney burst the surface with eyeballs buggin', reliving the excitement, grinning and nodding, *That old bitch can't aim worth shit!* We idled on the surface at trolling speed, talking, and for the millionth time wondered which of the fathers might be our father. It's always a short discussion. Like all children of parents who are swingers, we are forever mama's boys (or girls). I thought to myself, *How does a guy help his troubled cousin?* I remembered something Bertie told me, so I tried *Fathers? Bro, fathers don't matter, we are the ocean...all the rest is just current and tides.* Rodney gave me the eye-roll. To tell the truth, I didn't really understand what Bertie meant either.

Heading west a squall came on and the rain pounded and it felt good to get pounded. Side-by-side we cruised down the Strait. Rodney heard there was squid schooling over that way.

# LASSO MY HEART

What I remember is sometime around nine years old, it became plain: my family was boring.

Weekly visits to the piano teacher provided the kids with instruction, theory, and bouts of fitfull practice, but there was never any music going in our house. My father would buy a new one-year-old Dodge Dart four-door from Hertz every third year, then give his old one to Mom. An aeronautical engineer, he came home every afternoon at 4:30 and read *Aviation Week and Space Technology*, always on the same end of the couch. As a family we were constantly in training to expect the expected. An efficiency expert would have left with a yawning shrug after spending time with this group.

While Dad read *Business Week*, Mom would work her way through the family's favorite recipes, most clipped from *Sunset Magazine*. On Wednesday, porcupine meatballs served with mandarin slice orange Jell-O rolled and wriggled on the table. Saturday saw the three kids puzzling over the not-quite-understood smell of Texas Hash. Sunday was Mom's day off, with guest Chef Boyardee making an appearance on the box of instant pizza. The rotated meals never fell on the same day of the week, unless the first day of the month was the same two months in a row.

While our 1960s American automaton family was playing to the strength of my father's left-brained-ness, I began to see indicators that my mother, Hazel, was not showing all her cards. I first caught her doing the soft shoe in the kitchen to the hiss of the pressure cooker while making Swiss steak. How had she kept this from me for nine years?

Other discoveries cropped up. Hazel took up mid-week skiing with her girlfriends and bought an outfit rivaling anything Jackie O. might have worn at St. Moritz. Charcoal drawings of "life models" were found tucked into the *Idaho Gazetteer*. Aunt Winne visited and asked if Hazel might play the solo from Jimmy Dorsey's hit *Besame Mucho* for us on her sax. *On her sax?* said our six eyes as they shot over to Mom. While Dad tended to his relationship with the cedar gutter repairs, Mom had Bill Evans hidden in a Perry Como sleeve. The evidence piled up. Hazel's predictability was beginning to look like a front. A week earlier she'd shouted "SHIT!" when I said I'd forgotten my sheet music as we pulled up to the piano teacher's house. Coming from my mother, this was a very weird Tourettal outburst.

But it was my discovery of Hazel's relationship with the vacuum that tied the clues into a knot. Oblivious to me lying on top of the furnace register reading the comics in the living room, she plugged her partner into the outlet. They started swiveling in and out of a two-step kinda thing, dancing to some honky-tonk tune only she and the Kirby could hear. Where a legged partner might have led *her* into a twirl, Hazel was the one leading these four tiny wheels with a flourish that left a paisley pattern on the avocado wall-to-wall.

How those damn Chinese ribbon dancers ever got into the Olympics I'll never know, but they had nothing on Mom and the vacuum cord. She threw the rubber line up into a sine wave-like serpent, arching up, and back, and while it was in the air, with the slightest twist of her wrist she'd tame the reptile just before it tried to slither out of the socket. Wielded like a fly line lariat, with complete disregard of the U.L. rating, this was art. Finished, they hovered together near the closet, Mom panting, the vacuum with its belt smoking, sharing their moment.

My father died this year. We knew he was a hoarder, but unlike most, every distributor wire, cotter pin, and bent drapery rod was labeled as to its history and connection to the whole of life. As we closed down the family house, my sisters, Hazel, and I were joking about who was going to get what. I told Mom the only thing I wanted was the cord to the Kirby.

*Author Intro*

# BETHANY LOY

I am a budding author working to explore the human experience. In my free time I enjoy video games and learning how to cook. I hope to publish thought-provoking pieces in the future.

# THE OUTERMOST SEA

Like a second sunrise, Alicia's house appeared over the horizon. It was all painted sunflower yellow. The house, the mailbox, most of the flowers in her garden, they were all that bright yellow, just a shade off from the edge of a flame. She must have been obsessed with the concept. I've never cared for that bright shade, but my friend made it work. When it came to aesthetics, she could make just about anything work. Maybe even me.

I blew a few strands of wavy brown hair out of my hazel eyes. It gets curly if I let it, so I keep it short, but I hadn't had a proper haircut in a while. As I pulled up, I took a moment to check myself out in the rear view mirror. The sunny weather caused my freckles to pop.

My grandfather always joked that one day my entire face would become one giant freckle, and sometimes, when summer came and the facial invasion was in swing, I almost believed it.

I'd been selling my youth for not nearly enough money, working a frustrating job on the other side of the rocky mountains, trapped in a paycheck-to-paycheck prison that left me without enough money or time to grow. But now that had all changed. I just packed up and drove over to Port Angeles, Washington. Alicia, a professional photographer I'd met at a party years ago and kept up with online, had invited me to stay with her one night when I was venting about my situation to her. I jumped at the opportunity.

My friend stepped out of her home to greet me. Her sleek black hair was tied in a loose bun atop her head; her suntanned skin made her light blue eyes that much more apparent. She stepped towards me in long strides, her

Amazonian build giving her the confident aura of a warrior in heels. Blue jeans ripped fashionably so the knees could poke out, a yellow blouse and a jean jacket completed the image, making me feel a little underdressed in comparison.

I stepped out of my car and shut the door. "You dressed up that nice just for me?" I asked, glancing down at my unkempt black sweatpants and band tee.

She, with a broad smile plastered across her face, sprinted up to me at a speed I could never manage in those heels, wrapped her arms around my shoulders and squeezed me in a generous hug. I squeezed back.

"Glad to see you made it here safe, Ruby," she said and released her embrace.

"Me too," I said, giving her a wide smile in return. "The guy on the freeway who nearly merged into my passenger door wasn't any help with the whole safety thing."

She laughed, "Yah, that isn't helpful."

She looked past me and peered into the windows of my old sedan, filled to the brim with boxes containing my every earthly possession. "Is it all right if you keep your stuff in there for now?"

I raised an eyebrow. "Why?" I asked.

She sheepishly scratched her head and looked away. "I kinda reserved ferry tickets to go to Canada today."

"I drove six hours to get here, and you're taking a trip to maple country?" I asked.

She waved her hands in a placating gesture. "It's just a day trip, besides," she tilted her head to the side, "You're coming with me."

I pointed at my sweatpants and said, "Not going anywhere looking like this."

"Of course you aren't," she replied. "I have an outfit ready for you."

My eyes widened, "Oh no..."

She put a hand on her cheek and beamed, knowing I was at her mercy. "Let's just call it a down payment on your rent. I have a cute dress that is too small for me, and I need some photos for my blog."

"Listen, I'm pretty tired and being on a ferry will be uncomfortable-" I cut my sentence short.

Alicia was doing her best to give me a pitiful pleading look. She clasped her hands together and pouted her lips, "Please, if you come I'll buy you a Beaver-Tail."

"A Beaver-Tail?" I asked.

She leaned closer to me like she was telling a secret. "It's like a Canadian Elephant-Ear, but fancier," she said.

My imagination kicked in, and I began to salivate.

Alicia knew she had me, but I played it off nonchalantly. "If you really need me, I'll come."

She flashed her teeth in another bright smile, then reached out and grabbed my hand. She began leading me into the house, "Let's go, let's go, we only have an hour to get ready."

"Isn't that enough time to get my stuff?" I asked.

"No, no, no, there's barely enough time to fix your hair. This is a good neighborhood; your stuff well be fine," she said, as she opened her front door.

\* \* \*

The bright yellow dress waved and flowed behind me in the breeze, as we headed for the ferry. We passed the Feiro Marine Life Center, and I made a mental note to myself that

I should visit it sometime soon. Maybe seeing the creatures of the deep up close would help alleviate my fears of the ocean's unknowns.

My hair was still a mop of curls, but it no longer strayed into my eyes. Alicia had put a white hair band on me to push my curls behind my ears. I glanced down at the midi dress that cascaded down just below my knees.

I stared at the white flats with yellow ribbons, then sighed, "I'm sure this get-up is nice, but it's not my thing."

Alicia shook her head disapprovingly. "I think it looks great on you, but you only have to wear it today at the most." She lifted up the professional camera strapped around her neck. "I just need the pics, and we'll be hunky-dory."

Alicia was fast walking the rest of the way to the ferry, and I struggled to keep pace with her. We entered the building, went through security, and found our way aboard the massive ferry just in time for the captain to blow its booming horn. The journey began.

My friend convinced me to warily approach the front deck and lean over the railing to view the waves. My heart fluttered with anxious fear, but as the ship bobbed with the water my fears calmed a little.

I couldn't help but smile, as my fear slowly faded and Victoria, Canada came into view.

* * *

Alicia and I walked the streets of Canada, my first time in another country. I'd always imagined my first trip would be more drastic, visiting a culture completely alien from mine.

My companion made good on her promise of confectionery Beaver-Tail. We ate the frosting-covered treats and sauntered around the city, only stopping to look at a display of souvenir bottles of maple syrup or a street performer.

We continued walking in the warm summer sun for quite some time. Then Alicia took my hand in hers and pointed towards a thrift store ahead of us. She began making a beeline for the building, pulling me along with her. Before I could even get the name of the place, we burst through the doorway and entered a maze of second hand clothing.

As tall as my friend was, the shelving was even taller. After she let go of my hand, I tried my best to stay close to her; I knew I'd lose her if I didn't keep her in sight. She excitedly ran her fingers through the attire, every so often taking a shirt off a hanger to better examine it.

A few minutes later, we found ourselves at the back of the store. This portion lacked the florescent lighting of the rest. It was dimly lit with a mannequin at the end of the lines of shelves. Alicia gasped and nearly leapt for the mannequin. It was adorned with jeans, a t-shirt and a blonde fur coat.

"That's perfect!" Alicia said, as she removed the fur coat from its display.

"For what?" I asked, looking over the puffy coat in her hands.

"Your outfit; this will give you a retro vibe," She answered.

I raised an eyebrow, "Oh will it now?"

She rolled her eyes at me, then she checked the time on her phone. Her eyebrows shot up. "We need to go, our ride back is leaving soon," she said. She sprinted towards the cashier desk with the coat in her arms, and I trailed behind her. Frantically she paid for the item, and we jogged back to the ferry. We made it with only a few moments to spare.

Once we boarded the boat started chugging along, slowly returning its passengers to the USA. As the sun began setting, Canada's shores receded into the distance. Standing on the deck, we stared at the brilliant orange and reds of the sunset.

Alicia said, "This is exactly what I was waiting for." She turned to me with the fur coat in her hand. "Quick, put this on and lean against the side railing."

I reached out and grasped the fur coat; it was incredibly soft. I raised an eyebrow. "It looks okay, but aren't you supposed to clean thrift stuff before you wear it?"

My companion rolled her eyes. "Just do it for the photos; my followers will go nuts for this."

I glanced skeptically at the coat, then back at her.

"Come on! Look at this! The boat, the wind, the ocean, the sunset and your outfit, it's perfect! Please, Ruby think of the aesthetics," she pleaded.

"Alright, alright," I began sliding my arm into one of the sleeves, "for the aesthetics."

"Awesome!" she said, turning on her camera and messing with the settings.

I slowly donned the coat as I walked to the side, then pressed my back against the metal railing. Glancing down, I saw the water flowing by at a surprisingly quick pace. The ship rocked slowly up, then dropped down. I struggled to keep my footing as the waves got more intense.

"Alicia, I'm not comfortable this close to the rail." I said, my voice shaking a little.

She aimed the camera and looked through the viewfinder. "It's safe, lean further back. Act like you're enjoying the wind blowing through your hair."

I reluctantly leaned back, as another wave lifted the ship up. My stomach somersaulted, and my hands began to tingle. I heard the sounds of the camera shutter clicking. "You got the pics?" I asked.

"Almost perfect, lean back just a little more. You need to look more relaxed."

I tried relaxing my face; I wanted to grimace. "I don't think I can lean any farther." Apparently I didn't listen to myself, because I leaned out even farther, inching my center of gravity out until, my whole upper body was past the rail. I heard another few camera snaps and relaxed, assuming she was finished.

Suddenly, I felt the ship rock upwards.

I reeled backwards and Alicia was falling away from me, just tilting backwards in slow motion. As she finally left my view, the realization hit me. She wasn't falling. I was.

With that understanding, time sped up and I was launched off the side of the ferry. I only had time to clench my eyes shut before I splashed into the freezing water.

The slap of the ocean against my body sent me into shock, and I rapidly sunk farther into the darkness. Waves rolled off the ship and tossed and turned me about.

I struggled to swim, but I was so discombobulated I couldn't tell which way was up. Clawing my way, I finally broke the surface and gasped for air.

Opening my eyes, I frantically whipped my head around, trying to make out where the ferry was. My mind raced with fear.

A booming wail sounded behind me, and I snapped my head towards it. I saw the ferry. It slowed to a stop, and I could make out the call of an alarm over the sound of the crashing waves. They'd stopped for me, thank god.

I tried to kick my legs, but something wasn't right. A cold dread ran down my spine as I thrashed about in the water, but my legs felt glued together. I tried swimming towards the ship, but when I brought my arms forward what I saw instead was two black, leathery flippers on either side of me. Something was trying to grab me!. I gasped and sank back down into the water, thrashing wildly to push away from whatever monster was trying to wrap around me.

Breaching the surface and gasping for air, I yelled for help, accidentally swallowing salty sea water in my panic. I coughed and tried screaming again, but something was off with my voice; it was much lower.

The sunset was fading; it was getting dark. I flailed my arms like a windmill, desperate to reach the ferry.

Then I saw my arms, and stopped in shock, sinking back into the water. My mind went blank. I couldn't comprehend what I was looking at. The flippers I had seen earlier... those were my hands.

Heart skipping a beat, I looked down at the rest of my body. At first it looked like the blonde fur coat I'd been wearing had somehow gotten long enough to cover my legs. I flopped a flipper at my chest as I tried to take it off, only to find out that it wasn't a coat anymore at all; this was my fur. My legs were fused into a thick furry trunk, and my feet had become two flat flippers that stuck out the back of it, pointing to either side.

*What was I? Was I human anymore?*

The ferry lit a spotlight and they started scanning the water. I turned and swam towards the light, yelling for help, but my voice came out in gruff barks. The spotlight swung towards me and I flinched back, blinded. It stayed on me for only a few moments, then it began searching again.

*They don't know that I'm the person who fell overboard,* I thought.

The sea sloshed me around and my muscles tensed. I didn't want to be here. I needed to get out of the water!

Frantically swimming towards the ship, I barked and barked, hoping anyone would notice me. I came up beside the ship and slapped the side with my flippers, trying to get the crew's attention.

The boat began to move again, and the sudden pull of the propellers dragged me under. I fought against it as best I could, however the force was overpowering. I spun wildly around in the dark, watery abyss.

I felt my strength slowly leeching out of me, then suddenly my awareness was swept away, my ears no longer hearing the crashing sounds of the ship fighting against the sea, my limbs no longer feeling the cold grasp the icy water had on me. Each sensation was stripped away, and I was left in darkness.

And before long, the darkness slipped away from me as well.

\* \* \*

My head ached, but I felt really warm. My face was in the open air. Slowly waking up, I felt a pressure on my chest. Sitting vertically in the water, I flexed my hind flippers a little. Now conscious of my bodily position, I cautiously opened my eyes.

I saw the early morning sky, the darkness slowly fading with the rising sun. My predicament nagging at the back of my mind, I attempted to keep myself calm. The pressure on my chest moved a little, and I froze in fear. Cautiously I lifted my head out of the water and looked forward.

Two glowing green eyes stared back at me, and a cold shock ran through my spine! The pressure on my chest was this creature pressed to me. My heart went wild, frantically beating in anticipation of attack. I pushed the being away, and began to swim in the opposite direction. I heard splashing behind me, and I waved my flippers as hard I could.

How do you escape something in the open water?

This was some kind of nightmare; whatever kind of stalking fiend this was, it was going to overtake me, and I would fall prey to whatever pursued. I kept wriggling my new body trying to swim, when another set of bright eyes rose from the dark water in front of me.

I veered to the right and swam as fast as I could. Suddenly I slammed into something that rose up in front of me. I somersaulted in the water, my stomach aching from the blow. Before I could flee again, a snarling mouth came into view. Razor sharp fangs coming towards me, I cowered back.

"Watch where yer goin' yah moron!" the mouth growled.

"She was frightened, give her a break," a voice said behind me.

"Don't give a 'damn about some frightened faker," the mouth replied.

A small brown seal swam between me and the fanged mouth, "What do you mean faker?" the brown seal asked.

The morning sun rose higher and began lighting the water. Blinking, I observed the beings around me. Directly in front of me floated the young brown seal, looking barely past being a pup.

The angry speaker in front of him was also a seal, an old light grey seal mottled with dark grey spots. His body was covered in battle scars and fat rolls; it was clear he was past his prime. He pointed at me with a weathered flipper, "Not one of us. She's human."

The young seal turned to look at me, tilting his head as he looked me up and down. He squinted. "No. She's my mum."

Taken aback I couldn't help but say, "W-what?"

The young seal ignored me and looked past my shoulder, "Blonde seals are rare and you said mum was blonde, right?"

A voice answered behind me, "Well yes, but just because one is blonde doesn't necessarily mean that specific yellow seal is your mother."

I flipped around to see the speaker, an adult seal. He had black fur, with light grey spots. Compared to the older seal, this one looked far more fit. He swam closer, and stopped beside us.

"Back to what you said, in what world is she human?" the black seal asked.

"Yer too young tah see it, used tah be a lot more a' them swimmin' around," the old seal said.

The youngest seal looked me over, then swam around me. He was looking closely at my fur. He glanced back to the elderly seal. "Nope. Seal," he said, waving his flipper towards me.

The older seal shook his head in disapproval, "She's just wearin' a skin," he said.

Something in my mind clicked, "Like a selkie?"

"Aye. Like yah aren't aware of what yah are," the grey seal glared at me.

The coat, that blonde fur coat was a selkie skin? If the myths surrounding people turning into seals are true, what of the other myths? My mind raced for a few moments. I rubbed my head with a flipper, trying to focus on returning to land.

"I didn't know this was a skin before I fell in the water," I said.

The black seal's eyes widened. "You're not saying he's speaking the truth are you?"

The brown seal tilted his head. "My mum's a human?"

"Sea witches bring trouble. Yah need tah leave before yah attract misfortune," said the elderly seal. He turned around and slowly began to swim away.

"Wait, I need help finding land," I said.

The old seal whipped around and snarled in my face, his lips pulling up over his long fangs. "Why'd I ever help a human, least o' all a skin stealin' one?"

The black seal pushed me out of the way, putting himself in front of the older seal's wrath. "Your current behavior is uncalled for." He stared the elder down in defiance.

"If yah had any idea what humans were really like," the elder said.

"What are they like?" the younger seal asked.

The elder sighed and glanced at me, "Selfish and troublesome, if yah had any brains-" His sentence cut short, his whiskers twitched and his eyes widened.

"Hide. One of those beasts is comin'."

The other two's whiskers twitched in response. They began to swim for the sea bottom.

I looked on in confusion, but then the brown seal wrapped his flipper around mine. "We need to hide among the weeds and rocks! Come on!"

I followed him down into the forest of sea plants reaching up from the floor. We then pressed ourselves into the crevice of a large stone together. Cautiously I looked around. Ahead of us I spotted the other two seals curled under a sunken log. The small seal nervously pushed himself against my chest. My mind flashed back to when I awoke; when I was unconscious he had been hugging onto me like this.

A dark shadow blotted out the sunlight. A cold sense of dread filled the surrounding water; it seemed like even the few sea anemones littering the sandy ground were cowering in fear. Slowly glancing up, I held back a gasp.

In its deadly tuxedo pattern, the apex predator, a killer whale swam above us. I was at first taken in by its beauty, but I remembered what these beasts hunt and pressed myself even more firmly against the rock. The brown seal quaked in fear, his eyes locked on the approaching threat.

After a few more dangerous moments the whale swam away and light returned to the seaweed forest. The black seal, the bravest of us, slipped out from under the log and scouted for threats. Then he looked to us, nodded, and we left our hiding spots.

Grouping back together and nervously glancing around, I asked, "How do I get back to land?"

The black one turned to me. "You really think you're human?"

"I know I am; please I need help," I answered.

The youngest seal swam up beside me. "Do you really need to go?" he asked, looking at me with sad puppy dog eyes.

I couldn't help but smile. "I belong up there." I pointed upwards.

The brown one twisted upside down and pressed his flippers together in a pleading manner towards the black seal. "Please help mum."

"She can help herself," interrupted the old seal.

The black seal glared at the old grey one, then turned back to the brown one with a smile. "I'd be more than happy to help."

The elder huffed and rolled his eyes, then turned away from all of us.

"Thank you, thank you," I said, my queasy stomach easing up a little.

"Land is only a few minutes that way. I'll lead you there," the black seal said.

The brown and the black seals began swimming forward, motioning me to follow. I looked back. The elder seal followed not far behind.

"My name's Ruby, by the way," I said.

"You have a name?" the youngest seal asked.

I frowned, "Don't you?" I said.

"Names fer humans," yelled the elder behind us.

I glared at the old seal, "Watch it or I'll give you a name."

"Do your worst, sea witch," the elder said.

I waved my flippers dramatically and said just as theatrically, "Henceforth, you shall be referred to as Uranus."

The grey one wrinkled his nose in disgust, and the black seal laughed. The youngest gave me a nonplussed look, "What does that mean?"

"It's a planet," I answered.

The brown seal's confusion didn't leave him.

The black one turned to him. "It's like a star; it's one of the worlds of the outermost sea," he said.

The brown seal's eyes widened in wonder. "I want to be named after the outermost sea." He looked at me expectantly.

I was put on the spot and gave a moment of thought to it. "How about...Pluto?"

Pluto somersaulted excitedly around us. "I love it!"

The black seal laughed. Then Pluto said, "And what about him?" pointing towards the black seal.

"Hmmm," I mumbled, taking a moment to think. "Mars?" I suggested.

Mars smiled. "Very good," he said.

We all continued forward, and I could see the shore approaching. I was finally going to get out of here. I glanced to Pluto, then to Mars.

"Why does he call me mum?" I asked.

Mars flitted his eyes from Pluto to me. "He lost her right after he was grown enough to survive on his own. We've been looking for her for a while." Pluto, swimming ahead of us, played and spun in the water. Mars sighed, "It's likely that she was preyed upon; blondes may be rare, but they're easy to spot."

Suddenly we heard a yelp from behind. Mars and I whipped around to see Uranus hurrying towards us in a panic. Behind him loomed a white splotch on a shadow, which opened a mouth bigger than the seal it chased, to reveal row after row of white teeth. The killer whale had returned, and we were about to find out how it earned that name.

"Pluto, the shore! Escape to the shore!" I yelled.

Pluto looked back in fright, and the sight of that monster put a burst of speed in his tail. We four raced for our lives, and the sea beast gave chase. It slowly fell behind, but it was an endurance chase, and I didn't know how much this strange new body could take.

Beneath us, the ocean floor grew closer and closer in what felt like a crawling pace. My heart raced frantically. Uranus, Mars, and I followed closely behind Pluto.

He must not have realized how close we were, because he suddenly slowed down to look back at us. That was a mistake; I slammed into the young seal and we somersaulted forward. Mars and Uranus in that moment rushed past us, their panic blinding them to our predicament.

Pluto floated a few feet away, holding his head in his flippers and rolling it back and forth. I'd ended up spinning past, so the whale made a beeline for him.

Something inside me snapped. I couldn't watch what was about to happen, so I charged forward, aiming for the giant monster's nose. I sped up to him, slapping his face with my tail as hard as I could.

That got his attention; he turned and snapped at me with his massive jaws, forgetting about poor Pluto. It chomped down on my right side with just a couple of teeth, and pulled away, trying to rend my flesh apart. What he got instead was the Selkie skin, pulling it partway off me.

And there I was, a human girl again, in exactly the wrong environment. One of my arms was still caught in the fur coat, which the whale had clamped hard in its mouth as it tried to shake me apart.

I couldn't breathe, but I had to fight back. With all my strength I kicked and kicked at the killer whale's snout. It shook its head in confusion, tearing me the rest of the way out of the coat and retreating into the depths.

My lungs burned from lack of oxygen and I rushed for the surface.

Vision fading, my limbs losing the strength to keep pushing me up, I wasn't sure I would make it.

Then I felt something under me, pushing me upward. A grey furry body with an age worn face. It was Uranus!

"Good on yah' sea wi–. Well, Ruby, I guess," were the last words I heard before everything faded to black.

I was found washed up on the shores of Port Angeles.

It took a while to get Alicia to stop sobbing and apologizing. I reassured her I was fine, and we got down to the business of actually moving me in and trying to move past the awkwardness of her almost getting me killed.

But as I settled in, I found my mind often fleeing back to the sea. I had to go back, I couldn't stop thinking of the wonder and freedom I'd experienced, and I needed to know Pluto and the others were safe.

The minute I was able to visit the shore, I did. I took long walks up the beach, keeping watch for seals and if nobody was near, I called out over the waves for Pluto, Mars, Uranus…any of them.

After a few weeks of this, I was beginning to chalk everything up as a near death hallucination. Then one crisp and foggy morning, I saw in the distance the form of a seal's silhouette, hidden in the mist.

I walked slowly, not wanting to frighten the animal. As I made my way through the fog, there sat a large brown seal, with a blonde fur coat in his mouth. He seemed to smile and give me a wink, before placing the coat gently down on the sand. Then he turned and began to shimmy towards the waves.

I quickly donned the wet coat and ran towards the water. "Wait for me, Pluto!" I laughed.

From the waves ahead, I heard Pluto respond, "Will you tell me more of the outermost sea?" He turned back to look at me as we slipped into the ocean together. "I have a pup that needs a name."

*Edited by Dalton Paget*

*Author Intro*

# HARLEY DAVIDSON

I was diagnosed with aplastic anemia at the age of eight requiring a bone marrow transplant. Because of this I have spent most of my life in and out of hospitals. When your world shrinks to fishbowl size, hobbies are a must. Since the beginning, a love of literature and language has been there for me both as a means of transport to an infinite variety of worlds, and as a way to document and process the events in my own.

In 2016 I started writing poetry at the request of my high school English teacher, Nellie Bridge, and I couldn't be more grateful for her influence. Now, at twenty-one, I am happy to carry this art form with me into a brighter, healthier future.

Harley can be reached at Astronobees@gmail.com

## ☉N IDENTIFICATION

> I've been thinking a lot about
dichotomies and Oreo cookies.

> Everything is bits and bites
one          or          the other
             A       B
why  choose  either?
        why  not neither?
> In choosing we sacrifice a dozen
In choosing none a choice is made.

> They say more people dreamed in
black & white before the invention
of color television.

parallel universes

> To separate, to divide, to compartmentalize
you on this side and you, yes You,
                    on the other.

> Computers may think in ones and zeroes
but we are not wires and circuits and
cold metal we are flesh and synapses
and red so much red hearts
hammering at the slightest of sounds.

> Life is bits and bites and
questions without answers
a choose-your-own adventure book
with only one destination
just pick a route and turn to

PAGE 3

> testing, testing, 1, 2, 3
results will determine your placement
a plinking plop radiating outward
for the foreseeable future


> please fill in only one bubble or
your test will not be    counted
given the choice between A and B
I  prefer essay questions, like


WHO
ARE
YOU
?

## BLUFF RAT GOTHIC

They say the locusts emerge once every 7
years. If you go out after supper and sit
on the old rotted planks of your front
porch and wait for the muggy evening sun,
that ever-permeable heat, you will hear
them. The roar begins under an orange
sky.
The RV Tourists: those weary
travelers seeking warmth—they are
trees without roots, tilting towards sunshine,
equivalent in all ways but one. They mistake
the roar for crickets; it starts slowly.
Then, unfurling into a chorus, a welcome
screech, suspended in mid air, wire-thin
and vibrating, with the land below. The
noise surrounds me like a blanket. It lulls
the whole neighborhood into dreams of cool air
and fiddle music.
Standing on the old
rotted planks of my front porch, wrapped
in a terrycloth robe, I clutch coffee.

The steam that should appear like breath
on winter days is instead dissipated into
the early morning air. The neighbor's
screen door creaks against the stillness. My
neighbor, the one who calls himself "Santa
on summer vacation," steps out onto his
rickety porch, wrapped in a terrycloth
robe, clutching coffee. We stare at one
another across the thin strip of dead lawn
that separates us, a strip of mirroring silver
separating reality from dream.
He scratches his beard, and speaks:
"So, didja hear the crickets last night?"

And so the mirror shatters.

# WHY

because we seek attention
wanna feel that thrum of positive
feedback in your respiratory systems
when other people smile and clap and laugh
the aspirations of an entertainer
or a lonely soul honing their craft
because we're screwed up
and wanna know if we're alone in that
(I say we because I am no longer
          lonely)
not sure if it's poetry slammed
or just a cleverly worded rant
because we see something beautiful in
all that, something true
and wanna know if others see it too
to show it to them if they don't,
share a moment if they do

I do art
because I'm not sure it's art
because I wanna be a part of
something greater than myself
those alchemists of history who
sharpened the skill of turning
feelings into ink
those people who make people think
adventurers hunting down beasts of
the mind and bottling  them for the
world to see
silly dreamers and over-sharers
all a bit crazy like you and me

and if that's art then so be it,
if that makes me a poet
I must speak before  I delete it

[insert

poem

here]

# IANO

(the inexorable march of days)

take me where it's the water we walk on
        and the land we swim
the land when time runs   backwards
        the days are fading golden
        the nights a cobalt blue
little boys sit playing tarocchi
in folding plastic lawn chairs
and old men race down the lane
pedaling like their driveway is the
Tour De France
where park benches take priority
and nothing ever matters save
the bees on the breeze
and the sun slowly cooking your hair
the music ever-present
no directions, all origins
only resonances remains
waves lick away marble
a thousand years it has stood
~~a thousand more unmade~~
a Sunday stroll beneath your feet
the bells cascade through man's
        created shoreline
each cathedral's ears are temporary

*Author Intro*

# JOHN VICTOR ANDERSON

A friend once advised treating author bios as dating profiles: Must love words. Must love music. Beaches may or may not be metaphorical, but the waves always mean something else. Holding hands may contain coded language. Or not. Playlists will spin more than songs, but also constellations, which eventually will help us find each other again.

I earned an MFA in poetry from McNeese State University and currently teach English classes for Peninsula College and the Clallam Bay Corrections Center.

Contact John at johnvictoranderson@gmail.com

# THREE THINGS

*There are three things you can never get back,*
my father always told me. *The spent arrow,*
*the spoken word, and the missed opportunity.*

He drew the song out with his fingertips
releasing words into the air for me to catch
—or try to. History too faint for me to hear.

Like his father before, he pantomimed
the words, honoring those gestures, important
as wilderness and path, father and son.

I still see the string of his bow drawn tight
against his eyes. Squinting, concentrating
beyond the sun, a mark I could never follow.

Setting aside the bow, he held up his open palms,
shrugged, waiting for the sound of a lesson
learned. I waited, too. I didn't understand

how hands so heavy could rein leather
tight as lightning yet fall soft and loose as rain.
Funny how all three things keep coming back.

## BLUEBERRY MUSHROOM CLOUD

### After a photograph

It wasn't just a some pie gone wrong song;
it was the history of an ordinary moment:
picnic hair bedazzled with blond summer
rain, fragile drops of light looping
the curls of gravity's golden thread,
those spins of your hair spun down, up,
and around, falling almost but not quite
over your eyes falling inward like a secret
best kept—or not. You knew even then.

I am caught, too, in the curl of this photo
even as I think of this photo: you,
a blueberry mouthful, bursting with pie
à la mode à la *yes* and *yes* and *yes*
spilling into your spoon, down your chin
as your Ring-Finger-Taste-Test dares me still
to not think about *this finger or my lips*
*or how you are sitting across from them*
*as close as this whisper*. But you are not
the only one who can dare across time:

I *Am* thinking about red, blue, your lips,
your finger, the way it would taste puckered
between my own lips. So *Yes*, my eyes stare
transfixed in this photo, still connected
to this one moment, *now*, focused on your red
lipstick melting into the lake of your spoon,
its bluing cream spilling into your lips spilling
into my lips: the aftermath of a sweet explosion
of more—such delicious fallout
fixed within your lipstick kiss, a signet seared
white into my memory, sealed like a promise,
the bluest blue waxing within the reddest red.
How should I open this letter from you to me
if not again and again and again?

# HUM

Some have theorized that it's the echo of ocean waves
colliding, or the tectonic movements of the atmosphere,
or vibrations born of sea and sky alike.
But if we could hear this music more clearly,
it could reveal deep secrets about the earth,
or even teach us how to sound out alien planets,
or one another, our many deep craters,
seemingly endless under these moonless nights
where we face one another without words.

Or, it simply could be the bee alighting
on your red shoulder, or the thunder
charging through your heart naked into mine.

# JOSÉ ARCADIO BUENDÍA'S
# MEMORY MACHINE

*It could not conquer death*
*in the end. He forgot*
*forgetting is a kind sleep,*
*a rest from the living's duty*
*to suppress. Our natural state*
*revises that old question of being,*
*to not be beholden to state at all.*

## I.

Strange a rose should open up itself only
fully by degrees rounded inside moonlit noons
while its scent recalls bud to bloom:
little Aetnas asleep, at once awakened,
the rush of divergent seasons,
the long, full-throated cry that splits
darkness and fire as so many years undone,
the leavings of recollections untraveled,
a winter's yarn pulled too thin, snapped
apart between spring's reckless fingers.

## II.

Your wine glass turned mouth-of-river lies easy
on its side, pours north a valley of unbroken waters
where our days spill from broken glasses
with other days spent upon their unbreaking,
unpuzzling patterns present then not, like you,
an afterimage of red. Placeholders
of color then, like my fingers drawing

lightly across your red smile. Or was that your hand?
My hand is not my own. It fades as quick as glints of river
water running through the drag of my open attention.

## III.

Who are we in the end
besides what we are left
between the fire and the darkness
burning but not yet burned?

## IV.

A single bud. A promise-token. Deposited
for future bank against time when I cannot see
the red folds of the rose unfolding. Strange
how its perfume paints for me still the red
of your fingertips hushing my wined lips dry,
teases my tongue down those whispered paths
lit only between thunderbolts made unmade.

# TAKING THE LINE

We've had lessons before on measuring,
my father and I, together squaring off
depth, height, and width, each right angle
cocked in front of one eye. Again
he rolls out the tape, reaches for the pencil stub
lost in his shirt pocket—the one with the hole
my mother never sees. Every other cut:
*Where is that damn thing?*
Sweat drips off his nose, dampens the 2x4's dust.

He holds that pencil like a brush, dragging
back and forth, pushing it forward along the edge,
wanting the line to take root deeper than the metal
made straight by fire and will, hands and use.
I hear the line drawn. Carved.
*Fifteen and a quarter short—take the line.*
I'm slow to stop staring at the lead sheen,
but I move like I know what I'm about. "Inside or out?"

My father cracks his back upwards,
wipes his shirt sleeve across his forehead
leaving black streaks of dust, like grout
filling in his own lines. He watches me
for a moment, glances down at the saw,
a gift, like the one his father gave him.

Its black grip fills my palm.
The balance, weight, feels right.
I trigger the power-switch,
and the saw blade moves like a child
who doesn't want holding.
It cuts the air, leaves its own line
as I plunge forward into soft pine,
taking the line even as I follow it,
not knowing where it ends,
and only settling sawdust and cut 2x4s
to tell me where he's been,

where I'm going.

*Author Intro*

# JERRY KOCH

I am an avid outdoorsman, having spent much of my life hunting, fishing, mountain climbing, scuba diving, whitewater rafting and enjoying nature. I've conducted geological research, explored for oil and gas in countries around the world, taught at the college level. With a Bachelor's Degree in Geology from Washington State University and Masters and PhD Degrees from Harvard, I freely admit I am educated beyond my intelligence.

My first book is *The Adventures of Huggy Bear the Raccoon*, and I have just completed the story of my Gold Star family in WWII, entitled *My Father, Myself.*

Contact Jerry Koch at bearpawpress@aol.com

# SUBMARINES SO CLOSE TO HOME

You can spend a lifetime hiking, climbing, fishing, hunting, clamming and crabbing in the wilds of Washington. You can even read its history in front of a fireplace on dark and stormy nights. But you still may never unearth how often the Olympic Peninsula was in the sites of Japanese submarines during WWII. Why? A lot was hidden from the locals by a government eager to avoid public panic.

I fit the profile above until researching my recent book, *My Father, Myself.* I came across a scruffy news clipping from the *Bremerton Sun* that my mother had tucked away. The headline:

## SUB SINKS SHIP OFF WASHINGTON COAST

According to the article, an American merchant vessel *SS Coast Trader* was torpedoed by a Japanese submarine on Sunday, June 7, 1945. It sank thirty-five miles southwest of Cape Flattery near the Strait of Juan de Fuca.

The captain and crew described the event. The torpedo hit about 2:20 p.m. Captain Lyle G. Havens knew the *Coast Trader* had suffered catastrophic damage and gave the order to abandon ship. The starboard lifeboat was badly damaged during launch and was unusable. But the crew successfully launched the port-side lifeboat and two large cork rafts. All sixty men escaped before the vessel sank in a matter of thirty minutes.

First Officer E. W. Nystrom and other crewmen in the lifeboat reported sighting the conning tower of a submarine two hundred yards from their location.

They stayed on the scene until the next morning when the lifeboat started to row for shore to get help for those in the life rafts. The lifeboat crew was rescued by the *Virginia I,* a halibut schooner out of San Francisco, and taken to the Naval Section Base at Neah Bay.

Just before dawn Tuesday, the life raft crew saw Coast Guard Aircraft V-206 circling overhead and fired an orange signal flare into the air. The pilot spotted the signal and directed the Canadian Corvette HMCS (K-106) to the rescue site. The survivors were brought to Neah Bay after "splicing the mainbrace" with issues of rum (an order given aboard naval vessels to issue the crew an alcoholic drink). By that time, the survivors, cold and wet, had been on the rafts for forty hours.

Out of the *Coast Trader's* crew of fifty-six, which included nine officers, twenty-eight men, and nineteen U.S. Army armed guards (deck gunners), there was one fatality.

The first officer described a 'surprise' he and his mates planned for the submarine if it came to the surface near the lifeboat. It was a 30 caliber Lewis machine gun he detached from the ship's bridge rail and carefully carried to the lifeboat in his arms. He took along nine drums of ammunition. As the explosion-stunned crew waited in the lifeboat amid the wreckage, he told them, "I hope I can get at least two Japs."

My research led me to more detail than the tattered article I found in my mother's scrapbook. The I-26 submarine that sank the *Coast Trader* was 356-feet long, one of the Japanese Navy's largest and most successful class of underwater boats, called "I-boats." They were fast, had long range, and even carried a small collapsible float plane which could be launched by a compressed-air catapult from the foredeck.

In 2010 a Canadian Hydrographic Survey vessel located what they believed to be the *Coast Trader* about two miles inside Canada's boundary, in approximately 450 feet of water. Images from their multi-beam echo sounder sonar showed a mass the same size and shape as the freighter. It appeared to be intact.

On June 2, 2016, underwater archaeologists, and a team organized by *Titanic* discoverer Robert Ballard, conducted a twelve-hour, live feed dive with a robotic submersible on the *Coast Trader*. Among their observations were the torpedo entry hole, a deck gun, and the ship's bell.

Ballard's videos clearly debunk the official explanation of an "internal explosion" sinking the *Coast Trader*, although that remains in the Navy's official record.

Reports of enemy submarine actions along the West Coast were generally suppressed by the U S government and "cause of explosion unknown" was often given as the reason some of the ships sank. But that didn't mean submarine warfare wasn't happening.

Like most Americans, I knew a bit about Pearl Harbor, the Doolittle Raid, and the Battles of Midway and Guadalcanal, and even Leyte Gulf. The eye-opener for me was how submarine warfare took part in all the above. And, in fact, nine Japanese B-class submarines prowled the West Coast from the Aleutian Islands to San Diego during 1941 and 1942.

For those interested in an overview of Japanese submarine activity in the Pacific, I've assembled the following list of events.

## PEARL HARBOR

On December 7, 1941, a day that will live in infamy, I was born...and Pearl Harbor was attacked by Japan. Two waves of aircraft, launched from six aircraft carriers, caused horrendous damage to ships and airplanes, killing 2403 Americans.

Each of five I-class submarines launched a midget sub early on December 7. Some of the midget subs were sunk by American destroyers, others were abandoned, and none did any real damage.

A third wave of planes to attack the oil tank farm was canceled. If the oil supply had been wiped out, American operations in the Pacific would have been delayed by more than a year. Not sending a third wave may have been a major Japanese blunder.

## DECEMBER 1941 WEST COAST ATTACKS

The I-26 was the first Japanese submarine in WWII to sink an American merchant vessel (this predates the *Coast Trader*). On December 7, it torpedoed the *SS Cynthia Olson*, about a thousand miles northeast of Honolulu, en route from Tacoma, Washington to Hawaii. All thirty-five crew members were lost.

In December of 1941, nine I-class Japanese submarines were stationed along the West Coast of the United States. On Christmas Eve, they lined up near lighthouses, awaiting the command to shell these critical beacons. The attacks were called off.

Speculation is that the admirals in Tokyo were afraid their valuable subs would be destroyed by American forces.

That attack could have caused enormous turmoil, diverting more men and materials to defend the West Coast.

Over a seven-day period (December 18 to 24), the nine Japanese submarines attacked eight American merchant ships. Two were sunk and two more damaged.

## ELLWOOD OIL FIELD BOMBARDMENT

Before the war began, a naval reserve officer in the Japanese Navy commanded an oil tanker, which he docked at the Ellwood Oil Field, California to take on a cargo of oil. While walking on shore, he tripped and fell on his rump in a patch of prickly pear cactus. The American workers laughed and taunted him. The egregious insult would not soon be forgotten. On February 23, 1942, the same captain stopped his submarine I-17 just off shore of the Ellwood Oil Field and fired 12 to 25 shells. The bombardment destroyed and damaged equipment. Even though his revenge caused only light damage, it was used to justify Roosevelt's internment of Japanese-Americans.

## A COVERUP IN BURBANK

Two submarine events created a concern that air attacks might follow. The two events were Captain Prickly Pear Cactus Butt's assault on Ellwood Oil Field and the sighting of a submarine just outside of San Francisco Bay. Steps were taken to protect the Lockheed Air Terminal and airplane production facility, (now Bob Hope Airport) in Burbank. With the help of several movie studios, the military covered the entire area with strategically placed camouflage netting.

From the air it looked like a rural subdivision. There were no air attacks.

## THE DOOLITTLE RAID

Four months after the attack on Pearl Harbor, Jimmy Doolittle planned and led what has become known as the Doolittle Raid. The goal was to show the Japanese they, too, could be attacked at home. He led sixteen B-25 Bombers that took off from the aircraft carrier Hornet and bombed Tokyo. B-25 bombers had never taken off on such short runways until the Doolittle Raid. This provided an important boost to American morale, even though little damage was done.

The submarine I-26 was in dry dock when one of the Doolittle bombs damaged a carrier in the adjacent dry dock slot.

## THE BATTLE OF MIDWAY

The Battle of Midway lasted from June 4 to 7, 1942, only six months after Japan's attack on Pearl Harbor. Their plan was to lure American aircraft carriers into a trap and capture Midway. It was also in response to the Doolittle raid.

American cryptographers discovered the plan, and the Navy prepared its own ambush.

The submarines assigned to detect the American carriers arrived too late to do the job. Why? Maybe they were delayed because more than one Japanese Naval Commander glorified surface fleets over submarines. Whatever the reason, without them, the Japanese had no idea where the American carriers were. All four of Japan's large aircraft carriers and a heavy cruiser were sunk, while the U.S. lost only the carrier *Yorktown* and a destroyer. This was a decisive strategic defeat for the Japanese Navy.

## VANCOUVER ISLAND

The I-26, patrolling north along the coast of Vancouver Island in British Columbia, shelled the lighthouse and radio-direction-finding (RDF) installation at Estevan Point near Tofino on June 20, 1942.

## FORT STEVENS, OREGON

The following day, the I-25 shelled the U.S. Army base of Fort Stevens at the mouth of the Columbia River, just five miles west of Astoria, Oregon.

The captain guided the submarine to the south, surfaced, then turned north past the brightly-lighted towns of Seaside and Gearhart. As they moved north toward Russell battery, the submarine was well within range of all the gun batteries. The first shots landed south of Fort Stevens and one just missed a house, creating a shell crater that is marked by a monument today. The last shell hit 1500 yards north of Battery Russell. It sprayed the direction finder station with sand and gravel. Of the 9 to 17 shells fired, none did any real damage.

After the attack was over the submarine crew made a horrible discovery. They were sitting on the bottom of the ocean. Although they were still in sixty feet of water, the minimum depth needed for safe operation, the outgoing tide had allowed freshwater from the Columbia River to pour into the surrounding ocean and replace much of the saltwater, which decreased the buoyancy. They had to stay there, as sitting ducks, waiting for the incoming tide and denser water to lift them off the bottom.

As the shells came in, Colonel Doney, the new commander of Fort Stevens, ordered the gun batteries to stand down and not turn on the spotlights. This was in spite of the fact that his battery commanders could see the submarine, had calculated it to be well within range of their guns, and were aimed at it. Colonel Doney was being badgered by the battery commanders to allow them to return fire, and he shouted over the phone that if anyone returned fire he would court-martial the entire 249th Coastal Artillery.

Gun crews reported that the submarine was visible in the same spot until 4:00 AM, yet no order to fire was given. The aftermath of the attack was ugly. The Army has never issued an official record of the events of this attack. The commander of Battery Clark was called in to explain why 25 of his men went AWOL. He said they were denied the opportunity to do what they were trained to do, destroy any enemy threat to the Columbia River Harbor.

It is difficult to believe that the first attack on the U S mainland by a foreign country since the war of 1812 was not answered by even one shot.

## BROOKINGS, OREGON FIRE BOMBING

The I-25 surfaced again, off the coast of southern Oregon near the town of Brookings on September 9, 1942. It launched its small floatplane.

The pilot, Nobuo Fujita, flew inland several miles, dropped a 170 pound thermite incendiary bomb, saw an explosion, dropped a second bomb, and returned to the sub.

Japan was unaware of how wet that season had been on the Oregon coast. The bombs didn't ignite much of anything in the damp woods, and the attack was a failure.

Twenty days later, the I-15 returned to America with Fujita and his plane, and they dropped two more bombs near Port Orford, Oregon. These failed to detonate, and the site has never been found.

Fujita and his family traveled to Brookings for a ceremony on September 9, 1962, on the twentieth anniversary of the attack. As a very meaningful peace offering, the pilot presented the city his family's four hundred year old Samurai sword that he carried with him in the plane on the original mission. He hoped that giving this valuable gift to a former enemy, in the finest of Samurai traditions, would serve to pledge peace and friendship.

The Japanese took great pain to avoid civilian casualties. For instance the crew of the sub said that during the night raid on Fort Stevens, it would have been much easier to bombard the brightly-lighted towns of Gearhart and Seaside than the blacked-out fort.

The Western Defense Command ordered a blackout in coastal towns in August 1942 that lasted until the end of the war.

## GUADALCANAL

On August 31, 1942, US carrier Saratoga was torpedoed by Japanese Submarine I-26, 260 miles south of Guadalcanal.

On November 13, 1942, during the Naval Battle of Guadalcanal, the cruiser USS *Juneau* was hit by a torpedo from a Japanese destroyer and slowly steamed away on the port propeller. The I-26 launched two torpedoes; one hit

*Juneau.* There was a huge explosion, and the ship sank in twenty seconds. Of the crew of 697, a little over one hundred sailors made it into the water. All but ten died from the elements and shark attacks, including all five Sullivan brothers. The movie *Saving Private Ryan* was about getting the other Sullivan brother out of the war in Europe, before he was killed.

Paul Allen, the former Microsoft executive who has financed ocean exploration, announced that his crew found the *Juneau* on March 17, 2018. Photos show details of the wreck including a gun turret and damaged starboard screw, as well as the functional port screw.

## BATTLE OF LEYTE GULF

On the night of October 25, 1944, in the aftermath of the Battle of Leyte Gulf in the Philippines, the I-26 was sunk east of Leyte, ending a reign of terror in the entire Pacific and Indian Oceans.

## THE USS INDIANAPOLIS

The review of Japanese I-boat submarines during WWII in the Pacific would be incomplete without mention of the sinking of the USS *Indianapolis*. During a secret mission, the ship delivered critical parts for the first atomic bomb to be used in combat, to the United States air base at Tinian. While on the way to the Philippines after the delivery, it was torpedoed by submarine I-58 on July 30, 1945. In about twelve minutes approximately three hundred men went down with the ship.

The remaining nine hundred faced exposure, dehydration, saltwater poisoning, and as they waited for assistance, sharks. It was the most horrendous shark attack on humans ever recorded. Only 317 sailors survived. The sinking of the USS *Indianapolis* was the greatest single loss of life at sea in the history of the U.S. Navy. In the movie *Jaws*, the sea captain who was told he 'needed a bigger boat' was portrayed as a survivor of the Indianapolis disaster and talked about his experience.

---

*Jerry Koch's book,* My Father, Myself, *features his research into the War in the Pacific, and the involvement of his Gold Star family.*

*Author Intro*

# MICHAEL MEDLER

I write because Nature wills me to it. I recently left a dystopian suburb of Seattle and retreated to the kneehills of the Olympic mountains, cut the cable, bought whiskey. Now I find inspiration from deep woods, less so from demons. Though they are there.

You can find my words on-line at *Dodging the Rain, Nine Muses Poetry, Whispers, Plum Tree Tavern* and other poetry zines and anthologies. My recent collection, *Boundary Points* is available on Amazon. My newest collection, *Cresting the Salish* is also available on Amazon.

Contact Michael at 1953mcmedler@gmail.com

# OF RAINBOWS AND WILLIWAWS

Open water erases seasons, shrouds knowing, bends color
to its own device. The sweet sting of warm rain burns
my already sun-blanched face. Spring storms rant,
raucous across a vibrancy of sand, of stone that begs

a wider berth and a tack north along cloud fronts
rends the sky with mainsail. Sea rips, broken on tide runs
where breakers loft frost and flotsam. Once-protected
island lees call down cold sky. It falls hard into close-

hauled sheets. My wet hands grip the wheel hard,
hold the lines 'til storm-break shatters, scatters shards
of cloud into seas of furious foam. An arc of hues,
of sun, fires flame across this early spring sky.

*A williwaw is a sudden blast of wind descending from a mountainous
coast to the sea. The word is of unknown origin, but was earliest used by
British seamen in the 19th century. -Webster's*

# PURL

She's fixed on language of her hands,
a clack-wrap of needle on wool,
on needle, her body still, nuzzled
into the curve of an armchair. Her

thoughts brim with a count of numbers,
ignore the TV news. Pursed lips bend
in a depth of focus, a shift of yarn
from side to side. The newsman

tells me of killings, of multiple egresses
from earth. She glances, refocuses
fingers, rocking fiber from needle to needle.
Clack-wrap, clack-wrap, heads on the screen

feign emotion, "our hearts go out...".
Clack-wrap, she starts another row
after bind-off and a glance at the screen.
Children in cages. A pink tongue wets

her lips as she pulls at selvage, pulls
at thoughts of unfinished lives, at suffering.
She would knit all this together if only
her fingers could work fast enough.

# WINDROSE

Make me a shadow in the dark,
a windrose devoid of cardinal points.
Break down hues to scour sunset,
sky silent as empty pages, each

pointing to where you hide. Don't
hint me into correspondence.
Fold words beyond torn shrouds
of mist, blue awaits your time.

Go westward, along a roseline
to where this late light fades, to
where green seas beckon the gift
of a day far beyond this crossing.

And after glow fades to spark,
you'll know I follow the chart,
rusted compass in hand. I beg you,
make me a shadow in the dark.

# TANTRUM

Storms promise to unfold.
Dull gray flannel rumbles,
cackles, holds hard as the sky
steps forward in anger, its chest

rent, its breath blowing billows,
bleeding sheets of rain. The crest
of distant ridges rends
fabric, a confident tear

where the sun sways. Zeus
growls, throws bolts -
a God-like tantrum. I descend
wet steps to the yard below,

gather damp-dry laundry
from dripping lines. I wear
godly colors, jeans folded
wet with regal care.

# SPENT

I'm the graded plot scraped into the north meadow,
the crooked boards of a barn door. I am the cross of red paint
on a tree trunk. Blackened with age, I am used, cut and buried.

I've learned a way to fall. The movement bends me to it,
has become the silent testament of how boards and joints work,
the slow grinding turn of one hard surface against another.

Lying alone in shadow, broken boards, spattered in red, I cannot
rise from this fall I am now become. There are hammer and nails
in the kitchen drawer by the sink, and the shovel is on the step.

# OLD GLORY

The day bends on certainty. Like the quick closure of a clasp,
a final grain from an hourglass, the bow of a ballerina at curtain
close, I follow each day to its end. I have declared my deepest

truth, abdicated the soil beneath me as I hungered for a greater
humanity, a human-ness that represents all, equally. My colors
have run with blood, split wide and fast from bullet holes,

listened to empty inaugurals. Where time has folded me,
offered to a widow after gracing her son, I must burn now,
cremated at some freedom rally so I may be "better defined."

*Author Intro*

# GRACE ROSEN

I am an artist, author, masters level counselor, educator and speaker committed to creative community collaborations. I've lived in Port Townsend four years, and have served three years as a private caregiver & co-owner of Peninsula Home Care Cooperative. I coach & counsel people concerning breathing, creativity or anxiety/stress challenges. I also offer breath and relaxation groups that foster oneness and peace within our community.

I have participated in Peter Quinn's poetry classes at Imprint Books. Inspired by my relationship with nature, inner awareness practice, dreams, I trust what comes through for me to create a poem.

My writing began in earnest 2002-2006 during my time in Dana Point, CA with writing coach, Elana Golden. A chapter from my manuscript has been published, "Forgiveness Beyond Time~ A Wider View of Family Murder. Gone Fishing" in *Where the Tree Falls, the Forest Rises: Stories of Death and Renewal* by Charlene Elderkin.

Contact Grace at NancyGraceRosen@gmail.com or
https://www.linkedin.com/in/nancygracerosen/ and
her website: www.purenergy.net/writings/yourbreathisaportal

# COSMIC RAINBOW SPIDER WEAVERS

Beautiful breezes caress as songbirds sing at dawn.
Inner dream vision reveals a power of the ancient grandmothers on
the move, rise up, crawling together as one
Gather to build a network, weaving webs of creative dreamtime.

The dream weavers are moving in mass, legions,
fields of spider clan
climbing up and out of the deep cauldron of space and time. Weavers
of the cosmic web within us
beyond our cognitive comprehension.

Their silence golden amidst deep darkness,
womb spaces of our Earth.
Our bodies' core,
a cosmic empty world of galactic space.

Each travel along a column of light,
emerge, surface to a collective coven, a way of being,
weaving a reality beyond space and time,
light and dark, good and evil.

Our presence fills with collective conscious awareness.
Frequencies of light sensual sensitivity and organic evolving essence
melts into, permeates our body and softens.
Surrendered to the deep flowing current of life living itself.

Pure energy emerges
beyond density of confusion, fear and tension.
Ancient shadow spiders rising up through our body
dissolve density to a subtle brilliance, bright as the sun

Become a dream weaver of dark and light,
no longer afraid of being consumed by the black inkiness of the void
where All arises.

While still living in Portland, Maine I had a dream that inspired the above poem. In my dream the grandmothers rise in unison, walking together, determined and swift, they walk along an inner tunnel of light. Black, brown, some spiders the size of tarantula. Climbing up into the light until they fill the entire column of light, till all I can see is deep indigo black and wake up.

I begin to contemplate the meaning and significance of this dream to me now. The power of their silent movement fills me with anticipation, eager to know where they are going? What draws them to the surface of the earth, what's their message to us?

Grandmother spiders symbolize for me, the depth of the divine yin flow. They embody resilience, an unstoppable conviction keeps them all moving together, a field, a force to be reckoned with. Such power and strength can no longer be denied, ignored nor feared.

Dream of Spider medicine, yin power, immortal, primordial essence.

*Author Intro*

# MARLENE SHINN LEWIS

Marlene Shinn Lewis is retired and living on Washington's Olympic Peninsula after 46 years in Alaska. She writes both personal essays and short fiction and has introduced and annotated the only modern edition of the 1867 play *Alaska, A Spectacular Extravaganza in Rhino-Russian Rhyme and Two Acts.* Marlene has taught English and Written Communication classes at the University of Alaska Anchorage and at Wayland Baptist University and is currently working on a novel-length work of fiction. She and her husband are Master Gardeners and volunteer for several organizations locally.

Contact her at Marlene.Shinn.Lewis@gmail.com
or Seqribbler@gmail.com

# A NOISE IN THE NIGHT

"There's the house."

"The two-story colonial?"

"Yeah."

"Is there a dog?"

"No."

"All dark inside. No street lights. So far, so good."

"Let's go, then."

"Right."

"Watch out for that stupid statue on the front step."

"Ouch! That one?"

"Shhhh. I gotta figure out this lock. Okay, got it. Cross your fingers the door doesn't squeak."

"Dang, it's dark in here."

"Close that door. You're letting in the cold!"

"Which way?"

"Over here. You have the tools?"

"Yeah. Right here."

"Okay, let's get this over with before anyone wakes up."

"Dang, it's dark in here."

"Look, you've done this hundreds of times in the dark. Stop griping!"

"Fine! Hand me the knife."

"What kind of slash is that? All wobbly."

"I'm tired. It's late."

"Did it open?"

"Yeah. Hand me the screwdriver. Not that one, the big one. Ufff, urrf, ouch!"

"Will you be careful! And stop making noise!"

"Do they have a cat? I'm gonna sneeze."

"I didn't check for cats. Hold your nose."

"This isn't going so well. I need pliers."

"Here. Can't you hurry up?"

"Haste makes waste."

"Oh, brother. How about 'Caught for naught'?"

"Here, hold that while I twist this off. Ufff, urrf."

"Almost done?"

"Ahhh-choo!"

"Quiet! Lucky for them they're heavy sleepers."

"Dang, it's dark in here."

"Done now? Okay, put everything in the bag and let's get outta here!"

"Careful of that coffee table."

"Ouch! That one?"

"Ahhh-choo! There's the cat!"

"C'mon. Get a move on!"

"I'm tired. It's late."

"We're almost done."

"Whoever thought it would be so hard to put together a *Ride 'em Cowboy Rocking Horse!*"

"C'mon, Santa, we gotta get to the next house. I scheduled a doll and some books. There's nothing to put together."

"Bless your little pointed ears!"

## A PROBLEMATIC PULITZER

While I was still shaking my head to clear it and figure out where I was, a little boy wandered into the room. It definitely was a room, although there weren't any features apparent. It definitely was a little boy, although *his* features were too apparent. Dressed like Little Lord Fauntleroy. Pale blue satin—good grief, *satin*?—pedal pushers and white stockings. They probably weren't called pedal pushers. Frills, lace, tons of it around his neck and sticking out his coat cuffs. Were those *jewels* on his fingers? Must be a costume party somewhere.

He bowed. "Hello. I'm Edward. I'm twelve. Who are you?"

"Last I checked I was Ken Miller. Where's your mother?"

"*Ken*. That's not an elegant name, is it?"

"Live with it, kid. Where's your mother?"

"Oh, here's Richard, my brother." A younger version of His Cuteness trotted in. Yellow, not pale blue. "Richard is nine," continued Edward, "so he didn't get to wear the crown. I did, for a day or so. I don't mind."

"Where's your mother?" I snapped.

"She lost her head some time ago, so she can't be here," Edward advised carelessly.

Not to be left out of this scintillating conversation, Richard padded over in his little black slippers and peered into my eyes, asking, "What did you do?"

Taken aback, I blurted, "I write. Books. Well, not any that have been published yet, to be honest. Mostly journal articles to keep a roof over my head."

"What did you do?" Richard repeated.

Before I lost the little temper I still maintained, we were joined by a polite gentleman in an understated gray suit, perhaps in his mid-thirties, although his brown hair was receding like the ebb tide. He smiled and turned to the kids. "Anyone interesting?"

"Not so far," replied Edward.

"Now wait just a minute, you dolled-up little rug rat—"

Promptly holding out his right hand to me, the gentleman smiled and his eyes sparkled impishly. "Hello. I'm afraid you haven't been welcomed properly. The boys get so bored, you know. You are—?"

Mollified, I answered, glancing sideways at the boys, "Ken. Ken Miller. I've been told my name isn't very *elegant*..."

He laughed outright. "That sounds like Edward. He can be prissy with strangers. Everyone calls me D.B.," and we shook hands like the proper gentlemen we were.

"Okay, D.B., where are we? I'm a little fuzzy. I'm pretty sure it was a mind-blowing party last night, but someone else will have to confirm it for me."

Before D.B. could answer, the room filled up with two loud, laughing men who tumbled in like St. Bernard puppies. They were costumed like cowboys and even smelled the part.

"Our bigger boys," grinned D.B. "Harry and Bob."

Thumping right up into my personal space, they grabbed my hands and wrung them in a parody of their costumed personas. Maybe it wasn't a parody; they seemed so earnest and downright happy.

"He's Bob, but you can call me Kid," enthused one. They looked and acted too much alike for me to care which was which.

"He's Harry, but you can call me Butch," the other bubbled with an ear-to-ear grin.

Uh oh, I think the costume party's ratcheting up here. Butch and Kid? No way was I going to ask the obvious question of Kid. I tried a more sober course instead. "You know, you two are the spitting image of Paul Newman and Robert Redford. But if you want more realism, Butch and the Kid were not nearly as nice or even fun. Do some research, and you'll see what I mean."

They looked at each other and then burst into louder laughter. D.B. and the little Fauntleroy twins laughed, too. One of them—either Butch or Kid—stifled his laughter enough to explain.

"We can't *do* research, we *are* the research, Ken. Then when we saw Newman and Redford in the movie—*our* movie—we decided we wanted to be like that rather than our old not-nice selves. We're having way more fun than we had before."

Butch agreed. "Why not? Who's to care?"

"*Stop!*" I nearly shouted. Okay, I did shout. "D.B., you seem to be the only sane one around here. Where are we? Who are these weirdoes and why are they in costume?"

D.B. looked a little sheepish as he glanced at the others. Then he addressed me on a more formal level.

"Ken Miller, we don't know exactly where we are, but we know *who* we are." Gesturing to the boys he continued. "Let me introduce Edward V, King of England, and Richard of Shrewsbury, Duke of York."

As each was introduced, he executed a graceful and, well, princely bow. Those were not twenty-first-century little boy bows. Then an appalling thought hit me.

"Your mother, Edward, my gosh! Marie Antoinette— you said she *can't* be here? If you don't know where you are, why can't she be here?"

D.B. answered for Edward. "Those of us here are enigmas to the world. Mysteries. Disappearances, unconfirmed deaths, unsolved riddles. History has never proven the fate of Richard and Edward, though there's plenty of speculation. Most people are convinced they were murdered. Some people are certain they were rescued and hidden far away, maybe outside England. But the boys know, of course."

D.B continued. "I'm popularly known as D.B. Cooper. Had no idea I'd make such a splash—pun intended!" He smiled. "It's not my real name but I'm comfortable with it now. History debates over what happened after I parachuted out of that plane. Only I know. It's a curious fact, too, that we all appear here as we looked when we disappeared, whether or not that disappearance led to death or many more years of living."

I'm sure my mouth was working like a hungry mindless trout. This was amazing! I'd finally find out the answers to questions that had baffled the world for so long. Butch Cassidy and the Sundance Kid! Wow! Were they really killed in a Bolivian shootout? I turned to Butch—or was it Kid?—with brows raised.

"Robert Leroy Parker and Harry Alonzo Longabaugh, but we much prefer our publicity aliases. How would *you* like to live with those names we were saddled with? Bank tellers would have died laughing. Hmm, maybe we should have tried that."

I was almost afraid to ask, but in the interests of research I plowed ahead. "D.B., how many of you are here?"

"Oh, thousands. So many disappearances unexplained, so many miserable friends and families left behind, never knowing. Some made the news, but most are just everyday people who never came back from the store with the milk they meant to buy."

"Could I meet anyone if I ask? Maybe Judge Crater? Amelia Earhart? And I *have* to know what happened to Jimmy Hoffa! Could I meet him?"

"Behind ya, sucka. Whaddaya want?"

I jumped. "Whoa, you *are* scary, Jimmy. So how could you just evaporate like that? Bobby Kennedy said you were the most powerful man in the country except for the President. How could you let it happen?"

"Yeah," Hoffa sighed in disappointment. "The strong survive and the weak disappear. I sure screwed that one up, huh. I'll let ya in on the big secret." Hoffa leaned over and whispered a few words to me.

*Every*one was wrong! I was the only one who finally knew the answer!

A book! Two books! A five-volume set! With all the information I could glean from these—what, people? shades?—it would be a blockbuster. The road to Pulitzer was paved with gold! The Pulitzer was mine!

Feverishly I worked my way around the room to get the answers the world would pay fortunes to know. There were a few disappointments, but in general I found out stories and details no one else could ever know except these people themselves. It was hard to maintain a professional attitude: I acted more like a kid in a shop full of free candy. It was so easy; no one hesitated to tell me everything. This was just the start. I'd come back for more once I had the abstract written for my publisher.

I was exhausted as the high tide of adrenalin began to recede. Turning to D.B., who had been such a help, I told him I had to get back to my computer while everything was still fresh in my mind. He looked at me curiously.

"Where do I find the door, D.B.?"

D.B. looked a little uncomfortable. "Ken, don't you know why you're here? Think back. What happened after that 'mind-blowing' party last night?"

A blast of raw memory hit me. I'd been pretty smashed when I left the party, knew I shouldn't drive. When a couple of guys offered to drive me home, I accepted gratefully. Buzzing along in my own little happy-world in the back seat, I never noticed where the car was heading. Until we pulled off onto the edge of a dark road halfway up the canyon. Before I could even put two words together, I was hauled out of the car, stripped of money, credit cards, house key, and dang, there went my Costco card, too. Something weighing approximately a ton smashed my skull and I felt myself free falling over the edge of the cliff.

I'd become a mysterious disappearance.

I was okay with robbery and murder, but the loss of that Pulitzer really hurt.

# MINUTES OF THE 19TH CENTURY
# BOOK LOVERS' CLUB

Present :    Tilly Kohn            John Fremont
             Felicity Brown        Elizabeth Marden
             Anna Pacquet          Vickie Strode-Cather
             Martin (Marty) Flynn  Jacquie Andressen
             Kim Park              Peter Kirov
             Blue Moon Logan

The first meeting of the 19th Century Book Lovers' Club was held on March 3rd at 1:30 p.m. in the smaller public meeting room of Town Hall.

The first order of business, which was New Business since we had no Old Business, was to decide on a name for our group. After several suggestions, it was almost unanimously agreed that The 19th Century Book Lovers' Club will be our official name, capitalizing *The* and omitting the hyphen between *19th* and *Century* as too fussy-looking. There was quite a debate over the apostrophe in *Lovers'* since some of the group felt that the club was a possession of the book lovers while others insisted that it was a club consisting of book lovers. They used the Department of Veterans Affairs as validation. Peter looked up Veterans Affairs on his laptop and found justification for omitting the apostrophe in Veterans Day but nothing about the agency name. The pro-apostrophe members claimed that the agency was in error for omitting the apostrophe since the affairs most assuredly do belong to the veterans. It was suggested that we send a letter to the government advising them of this oversight, but the idea was tabled.

There was no decision made about the apostrophe. Because I volunteered to be secretary and am in the pro-apostrophe group, the minutes will reflect the apostrophe.

The second order of business was to establish what the members wanted to read and discuss. There were so many proposals voiced at the same time, that the following list is incomplete. Here are the recommendations I had time to write down:

| | |
|---|---|
| George Eliot | Dostoevsky |
| Margaret Fuller | Flaubert |
| Chekhov | Whitman |
| Verne | Stephen Crane |
| Thoreau | Willian Dean Howells |
| Arthur Rimbaud | The Brontës |
| Manzoni | Twain |

José Maria de Somebody's name I didn't catch

A couple of members argued that we should read them in their original languages, but a vocal majority stipulated that the works would be read and discussed in English because all but those two members knew only English.

There was a great deal of discussion about how to choose the order of books to be read, many of the members believing that the determining factor would be how loudly they spoke. To avoid potentially overenthusiastic persuasion, it was deemed necessary to table the process of establishing a reading schedule.

The question about how often to meet and for how long was added to the tabled discussion about book order and schedule.

For us to establish authenticity for The 19th Century Book Lovers' Club, someone wanted to have T-shirts printed with clever literary quotes on them. The support for T-shirts appeared to be from the male members while the detractors numbered all the women. The idea of having some kind of something printed with literary quotes, though, was generally thought to be a useful and positive advertising statement for the club.

Ceramic mugs were briefly considered and then rejected as mugs are too small to adequately display enough clever literary quotes to make the cost worthwhile.

Canvas tote bags actually received everyone's vote, so a committee was formed to research cost while another committee was formed to choose several clever literary quotes for the bags. There was a question of color and design which was referred to cost committee. Would the committee choosing quotes be amenable to suggestions from other members? Well, yes, if there weren't too many and the quotes were at once recognizable by reputable literary individuals. What did they mean by *reputable* literary individuals? Forget the *reputable*, then. The cost committee wanted to know how much they could spend and who would pay for the bags, designing, and printing. As there were no satisfactory answers that the majority could agree on, the tote bag idea was tabled.

Someone noted how long this first meeting was and would all the meetings (however often they were to be held once that was decided upon) be as long? A few noted that they needed to collect children from school, and someone else had a dental appointment in fifteen minutes.

In the middle of the impending exodus, no one knew for sure which of the members voiced disgust with the entire business and declared that The 19th Century Book Lovers' Club was getting nowhere and probably never would. This was the only time during the meeting that there was immediate unanimous agreement.

Since there was no one left to plan a second meeting, the first and last meeting of The 19th Century Book Lovers' Club was concluded at 4:30 p.m.

Respectfully submitted,

Felicity Brown, Erstwhile Secretary

*Author Intro*

# LINDA B. MYERS

After a marketing career in Chicago, I traded in snow boots for rain boots and moved to the Pacific Northwest. I spend enough time ruminating in these woods and on these beaches to pop out a darn good story now and then. To date, I have published eight novels in a variety of genres.

I write a monthly humor column for the *Sequim Gazette* and love the activities in our regional writer community.

My selection for this anthology is the opening of my historical novel, *Fog Coast Runaway*. In the story, a young girl vanishes into the 1890s Oregon wilds. Hardened loggers, sailors, and wagtails scare her less than the family she must outrun. *Fog Coast Runaway* is available at local retailers, on Amazon (print and eBook) and at www.lindabmyers.com.

Contact Linda at myerslindab@gmail.com

# FOG COAST RUNAWAY

An Excerpt

## CHAPTER ONE

April, 1893

Adelia Wright had a case of the morbs. Her dog was dead, her Pa fuddled with booze, her brother a muttonhead. And now this. Adelia was bleeding.

"What a blasted time," she swore to nobody now that Shep wasn't there to hear her. What on earth was happening to her body? She had no one to ask...certainly not Pa who wouldn't listen or brother Wiley who would only taunt. She needed a mother's help with this mystery. The blood soaking her bloomers just couldn't be a good thing.

The closest female neighbor was old Cora Dixon who held school classes in her home. It was a mile trek through the damp forest to the west, toward the ocean.

Adelia couldn't go without a gift. She snatched up a bouquet of adder's tongue, trillium, and fawn lilies from the orchard meadow behind the cabin. Then she traipsed on her way, switching the flowers back and forth in agitation as she went.

Cora Dixon came to her door hunched forward on a sturdy branch that doubled as a cane. Her mouth tightened as she peered down at Adelia on her stoop. "Gracious, is that blood on your frock?"

Adelia shoved the bouquet to the old woman. "These are for you. Am I dying?"

"Don't be batty, child." A crimson blush moved up the loose skin on Cora's neck to land on her wrinkled cheeks.

"But you cannot walk around in public like this." She took the flowers and ushered Adelia inside.

"Your father still has that heathen, don't he? Can she not explain what is upon you?"

*If she could, I wouldn't be here,"* Adelia thought but said, "Lilac does not speak English, ma'am. Why am I bleeding from under my belly?"

Mrs. Dixon put the flowers in the soapstone sink, then fluttered her hands like a hatchling attempting to fly. "People do not talk about these things," she whispered even though they were alone. "But your menses have begun. I will teach you how to get your rags up, and then no more will be said about it."

The old woman showed the young girl how to make a belt from muslin strips with safety pins and how to create pads by folding soft rags. "Use flannel or cotton or whatever absorbent rags you can find. Wash them at night and keep them for the next time."

When all was secure, Cora Dixon shooed Adelia out the door with a final warning. "This will happen once a month until you have babies. You are a woman now."

"Have babies? I am a woman?" Adelia thought maybe Lilac would have been easier to understand after all.

"Menses come monthly until you marry. Then you keep having babies and breastfeeding them. If you are lucky, you may not suffer the curse again for years."

*Isn't that the beatingest thing?* Adelia did not feel much like a woman, nor did she have a firm grip on the process of babies, but she was most thankful her innards were normal. Still, bleeding seemed like an undeserved punishment for growing up. She wondered what boys went through, not that she'd ask Wiley about it.

A mother might explain it to her in more detail. But she'd never known her mother. As Pa told it, he'd come home from the lighthouse one day to find baby Adelia in her cradle, shrieking in outrage, hunger, and sodden clothing. Her mother had vanished. "Not worth looking for the whore," he often added when talking about her perfidy.

That was twelve years back. Wiley said it was Adelia's fault. He was four years older and claimed to remember their mother. And to miss her. He'd never liked his little sister, calling her a pestilence when Pa wasn't around to hear.

As she neared the cabin, Wiley yelled from the vegetable patch. "Where you been? You ain't even dug out the weeds."

"Appears you must manage it yourself. I have to help Lilac with the meal." Causing Wiley extra work was the only good thing about the week so far.

* * *

"You know where that ol' bitch of a dog come from don't you, girl?" Her father George Wright asked. They were at the table. Through the cabin's open door, early spring sun rays cut across the dirt floor and plank table in strong bands of shadow and radiance.

Adelia couldn't keep her eyes from glancing at the rug near the fireplace. Shep's rug, now empty. She fought back tears, unwilling for Wiley to see how she ached.

*You tell me she was a bum often enough,* Adelia wanted to snap at her father. But she settled for, "Yes, sir." George spoke right over her as he reached into the pot for another elk short rib. He poured the last of the liquor into his glass. "From that last shipwreck before the light was lit. That's where. When the dark and the fog lifted, they found her howling amid a dozen dead men on the beach."

"Yes, sir." Adelia couldn't remember her father ever talking about much of anything but the lighthouse when he was home from his three-month stints on it. She'd given up trying to interest him in her life.

"Bitch was the only living thing survived. Musta swum a mile to shore. Been the settlement bum ever since, surviving on handouts."

She'd heard her father's story before, how Shep's crew might have survived if Tillamook Rock Lighthouse, off the north Oregon Coast, had been completed three weeks earlier. But its lamp wasn't quite ready, so the ship had no warning light to keep it off the rocks.

Wiley pinched her thigh under the table and twisted until she cringed. "Know what she did, Pa? Fed that dog our meat when you were gone."

"We're not to waste food. Hear me, girl? You mind Wiley when I'm not here."

Adelia knew her father wouldn't remember giving her that order. He forgot a lot, getting liquored up pretty quick and staying mostly boozy for the two weeks before he went back to the lighthouse. There he had three months to dry out before his next leave.

"Seems strange to me, her just dying on the stoop like that," Adelia said, staring an evil eye at her brother. "Seems something must have happened to her."

Wiley sneered. "I suppose somebody could of strangled her. Old as she was she wouldn't put up much of a fight. I woulda put her out of her misery with the Springfield long ago, Pa, if you'd let me use it."

"Ain't gonna tell you again, boy. That gun stays right where I put it."

This time, Adelia sneered at Wiley.

George Wright pushed back from the table, signaling the end of the meal. But he still had his drink. "Was a terrible gale the night the *Lupatia* went down. Lighthouse crew heard sailors scream even through the raging storm. Sails slapped and rigging creaked. Commander was crying, 'Hard aport.'"

Her father was off and running. The tale might have scared her more if Adelia hadn't heard it so many times before.

"They saw running lights, then all went dark. By morning light, they picked out the remains of the *Lupatia* in the surf. Twelve of the sixteen corpses were strewn along the beach. The rest are out there still."

Adelia picked up plates and left the table quietly to join the Indian woman cleaning dishes. They called her Lilac since they couldn't pronounce her name. She didn't speak English, and they couldn't handle the Clatsop language. Adelia liked this one, but her father replaced his women fairly often. Chinese or Clatsop women. Adelia put an enamel pan of water on the wood stove to heat and listened to her father drone.

"A lighthouse a mile out to sea, helluva thing. First foozler who tried to survey it fell into the sea. His body was never found. Helluva thing. Makes a man crazy, living out there on a God forsaken rock that wants you dead."

*You ever listen to yourself?* Adelia figured it was the lighthouse that made him daft. He'd been an assistant keeper for years on the light they nicknamed Terrible Tilly. That had to knock a man off his chump.

In the dark that night, Adelia listened to the moaning and grunting of the Indian woman and her father. It was the only language they shared, as the bed frame squeaked along with them. They were directly over her in the cabin loft. Her bed was on the dirt floor, as was Wiley's, with a ragged curtain drawn between the two.

Lilac gasped.

"What you suppose he's up to now?" Adelia whispered to her brother.

"Shut yer tater trap, or I might come show you."

Adelia had seen animals mate so she had a rough idea of what was going on. It was hard to picture what humans did, though. She had no interest in taking part, especially with an all-fired ratbag like her brother. She rolled on her side to face the wall. In the morning she would go to the creek and wash the rags Cora Dixon had given her. Hang them to dry on a vine maple where her brother or father would never see them. She didn't think she could survive that kind of humiliation.

She wished Shep was at the foot of her bed, but that wise old dog, her only source of affection, was gone. She'd carried the shepherd's body from the stoop into the woods to bury, deep enough for forest creatures to leave it alone. What she felt was new to her. It wasn't sadness. That was a part of life around here.

This was intense grief. It hurt worse than a burn at the stove when fat exploded or when Wiley punched her in the arm. This agony was on the inside, slicing through her where she couldn't rub it or administer one of Lilac's salves.

Adelia used to be able to talk to Wiley, when they were little enough. Before he became such a bully-boy. Had he killed her dog? If she could ever prove it, she'd use Pa's

Springfield on him. Maybe not to fix his flint for good, but at least to scare the bejesus out of him. She had to find where her father hid the ammunition first. She'd never admit it, but she was afraid of her brother now, every time her father went back out to the light.

Loss of her dog, mistrust of Wiley, and this bloody curse, all in one week. Life is a sneaky opponent that blindsides you whenever it chooses. Adelia was damn sure of that.

* * *

Two days later, George Wright left for his next three-month shift on Tillamook Rock Lighthouse. Wiley headed off to drink with friends or check his traps or whatever he did to get through the day. Adelia did not care as long as he was gone from her sight. She knew she was not really safe at home anymore. And she couldn't see things getting any better. Maybe she could make some money then leave. Sew or clean for other settlers maybe. She decided to work on a plan.

But time was not on her side. The next day, she was cleaning the coop, singing to soothe the chickens:

*Oh I went down South for to see my Sal*
*Play polly wolly doodle all the day*
*My Sally is a spunky gal...*

Her brother broke in with a liquor-slurred verse of his own.

*"Oh my Sis she is a maiden fair,*
*play polly wolly doodle all the day."*

A bolt shot through Adelia as she looked into his eyes, crazed with rotgut and lust. Wiley blocked the entrance. At sixteen, he was big, randy, and cruel. His shirt was filthy, his old boots smelled of manure from the field, and his pants of human sweat.

He smiled at Adelia, breathing out fumes of alcohol. "I'll show you what happens to maidens fair."

Her only weapon was the broom. She swung it at him, scratching his face. On her next swing, he grabbed the stiff straw, pulled the stick from her hands, and tossed it aside. Adelia tried to dodge past him, and nearly succeeded, but he caught one wrist, then the other, forcing her down. She yelled. The chickens squawked and flew in panic.

Wiley ripped through her thin bloomers and tried to shove himself inside. Alcohol impeded his finesse, and her struggle landed a knee in his groin hard enough for him to cry out. For a moment all was still, except downy feathers from the panicky birds flurrying like snow.

Then he started at it again, but the cocking sound of a chambered bullet stopped him. Wiley turned toward it, as did Adelia. There was the Indian woman, Springfield rifle in hand.

"You go," she hissed. Adelia realized Lilac had learned all the English she needed.

Wiley stood bent over, his hand in his groin where Adelia had kicked him. Blood trickled from the broom scratches on his face. He growled, "You will be sorry. You both will be sorry."

"You go."

He limped away. Adelia rose from the hard packed dirt. Her head was pounding and she couldn't catch her breath, but she realized she wasn't really hurt on the outside. Sore, scraped, and bruised but not really hurt. Bruises and scrapes were common as dirt.

Lilac looked at her and said, "You go." This time her voice was gentler.

Lilac was right. Adelia had to leave. They both did. Wiley would return. That knowledge curled like smoke around grief for her dead dog and fear of the unknown.

Adelia went to the cabin, put on her only other pair of bloomers, and packed an ancient valise with what little she had. She saw her brother's boots, the new ones he'd purchased with such pride. She tied the laces together then slung them over her shoulder. He would miss them, and she was delighted by that. Finally, she removed all the money from the old lard tin on the shelf. She gave half of it to Lilac.

Then Adelia left her home. She planned on never coming back.

## CHAPTER TWO

April, 1893

Adelia rushed along a deer path through the Douglas Firs and cedars. Blackberry brambles and maple vine reached out to trip her, but she ripped through them. Grief, anger, and fear fueled her flight. Although she'd never been fearful of the wilderness before, Adelia was spooked by every forest noise now. The idea that Wiley was trailing her, well, her heart raced even though she knew it was bunkum.

"Stop running and start thinking," she lectured aloud, willing herself to slow down and listen to her own reason. A mossy log that crossed a creek proved inviting, and she sat, dangling her feet just above the water. Tadpoles half-grown into frogs darted about in the quiet water below her. She took a couple deep breaths and listened to a pileated woodpecker hammer at a hole not too far away. Bees worked the Oregon lilies and lupine along the bank. A hive of wildflower honey would not be far away.

The sounds and scents drained her fear, soothing her enough to consider her situation realistically. Wiley was not thundering along behind her. He probably didn't know she was gone yet.

"And in truth, he is unlikely to come looking," she pronounced. A shard of grief for Shep sliced through her. Tadpoles and birds were no replacements at conversation.

Wiley should never want her back, on the off chance her father would believe her about what happened. "If he thinks at all, he's thinking good riddance." Of course, he might come after the money she had taken. She sighed at the puzzle. Then she moved to the next item on her mental checklist.

She needed a safe place for the night, somewhere her brother wouldn't find her if he did hunt for her. It took a while with her brow furled in deep thought. She picked a blackberry bramble from the end of her long ash blonde braid. At last, the perfect place flashed into her memory. "Let's go," she said, lifting her valise and heading onward. She wondered how long it would take her to stop talking to a dead dog.

It was another two miles or so to the old dairy barn. Its backside shoved up against a sharp rising hill so the door faced south, away from most winds. Adelia had seen it before when she passed this way. Wild rose bushes not far from the barn provided her cover to await the farmer who would no doubt soon appear to do the evening milking.

When he arrived he seemed a hardy fellow, cheeks and nose red above a massive dark beard of wildly curling hair. Adelia snuck to the outside wall of the barn and peered through an accommodating chink. The farmer burst into *The Old Settler*, singing to his trio of Holsteins as he began to milk.

> *No longer the slave of ambition,*
> *I laugh at the world and its shams,*
> *As I think of my pleasant condition,*
> *Surrounded by acres of clams.*

Except he modified the last line to *Surrounded by acres of teats*. Then he guffawed to his trio. Squeezing a teat of the cow before him, he shot a stream of milk to a ratter cat perched on her back haunches, awaiting her treat. Adelia clasped a hand across her mouth to smother a giggle, and the cows covered for her. They mooed for the farmer to hurry and unload their swollen udders.

As he left the barn, he called, "Good evening, Milky, Clara, and Clover. I thank you each for all."

Adelia watched while he moved the heavily laden pail into his cold store, deep in the side of the same hill that supported the barn. She did not know how cheese or butter was made, but she knew the milk would soon be one or the other. The thought made her hungry. Hungrier.

When she felt sure the farmer would not return that evening, she snuck into the barn. She knew these particular cows, having petted one in their pasture on an earlier day. Two rolled their eyes and moved away, but the mostly white bossy came close for a scratch around the horns then behind the ears. "Good girl, Milky," Adelia said, thinking that was a fine name for her. The cow gave her a raspy lick on the arm with a sandpaper tongue, causing her a second rare giggle. The others settled and accepted Adelia's presence. At least they didn't bawl for the farmer's attention.

She found a space between the barn wall and a pile of scratchy rope. She tamped down a small mat of clean dry straw, removed a horse blanket from a peg, and spread it over the nest. Using her valise as a pillow, she pulled her knees to her chest and covered herself with her cape. Her hidey hole was just large enough for a child, and when the ratter cat came to curl up there, too, Adelia was warm enough to feel drowsy.

Everything ached, spirit and body. When she thought of her brother, the ache spread in the way of a disease, building in malignancy. She was forsaken by parents and sibling, alike. She was a nobody, worse, a nothing. But that line of thinking would get her nowhere, and she whispered as much to the cat. Besides, the farmer had given her an idea. She now knew exactly what she would do the next day. A one-day plan was enough to help her sleep, that and the restorative power of a purring cat.

* * *

The growl in her belly awakened Adelia. It disturbed the cat, too, who stretched then disappeared on its early rounds. It was still dark, but Adelia knew she must leave before the farmer returned for the morning milking. She picked up her few things and replaced the horse blanket. In the process, her motion alerted the cows, who'd forgotten she was there. The two skittish ones mooed. First low, then loud. No amount of shushing appeased them, so Adelia ran from the barn, smack into the farmer. He held a lantern high, but dropped an empty milk pail and grabbed her wrist.

"See here, see here," he blustered in a startled voice, repeating it again as she squirmed. He struggled not to drop the oil lantern so close to the barn. Her wrist was very small and his hand very large. It was as if he couldn't quite tighten down so she slipped free.

Adelia ran with the speed of a young deer, her legs leaping through a field of new corn. It was dark, but she knew there would be woods soon, in any direction. Behind her she heard another "See here!" and plaintive mooing, then all was quiet except the chitchat of the earliest birds.

When she reached the safety of the trees, Adelia darted under a cedar, its lowest boughs dipping to the ground. She sucked down great gulps of air, thinking she was catching her breath. But the gulps didn't stop, nor did her eyes stop watering. Beneath the massive tree, the child mourned for the love she'd never had, for the few comforts she'd lost, and for the many fears she'd found.

But crying was a waste of time. It was a simple fact, and a childish thing she could no longer afford. She wiped her eyes on a dress sleeve. Adelia's stomach forced her out of her cedar den, its noisy protest for food becoming more important than safety.

She wondered what the farmer would think when he found the nearly new pair of boots she had left for him in the barn, the ones that belonged to Wiley. The thought brought a bit of cheer to her morning.

She was very close to the ocean, with small hill farms all around this stand of cedar and fir. As the sky began to lighten toward the east, she found a vegetable garden. It was too early in the year for most plants to mature, but she saw the shoulders of carrots that had overwintered. She grabbed four before courage failed her, and she ran.

It was her second theft, following the removal of cash from the lard can on the high shelf back home. She thought about how it felt, being a criminal, how she should be suffering deep shame. Certainly the reverend had taught her it was a sin when he preached at the church service held in settlers' homes, on days when there was no school. But when carrots tasted this good, thieving was its own reward. She wished she'd tried for some of the cheese she imagined in the farmer's cold store.

Adelia stayed close to the bank of Elk Creek following it toward the beach. It was wide here so it flowed lazily toward the ocean. She stopped now and then to skip a stone across the water or to braid fawn lilies into her hair, but she did not dawdle long. She wished Shep was with her. Distress bit her again. She simply must try not to think about the dog.

The stream led her to the south end of the new Elk Creek Road. The so-called road punched through the forest following an ancient Indian path. It was the only route over Tillamook Head, a bluff over a thousand feet high, dangerous where the ground was unstable at the coast. The road zigzagged up and over, eventually ending on the other side of the headland at Seaside, Oregon. Adelia's father followed this route on days he met the tender boat that took him to or from the lighthouse.

Elk Creek Road was a pair of barely passable ruts through a hundred jolting, nasty curves, and yet it was so much better than the preceding foot trail that a toll was demanded of anyone riding on it. If Adelia had a horse, it would cost her a quarter. If she had a wagon, she'd pay seventy five cents for the bone-jarring commute. *If wishes were horses, beggars would ride.*

She could ask a teamster if she could hitch a ride; that is what her father did. And there was an ox team heading out, hauling a load of butchered pork to the meat market in Seaside. But she was too worried that the driver might know either George or Wiley. Besides, she was far too reticent to approach a strange man: her luck hadn't been all that great with the ones she knew.

The sun was just rising. She quietly slipped out of the woods, around the toll gate and onto the road to walk the eight miles to Seaside. If she heard a wagon coming, she would disappear into the trees until the conveyance passed her by.

The first two miles twisted sharply uphill. Adelia began to sweat although it was still cool. In sunny spots along the road she found salmonberry shrubs with early fruit just ripening to orange, and she gobbled as she walked on. She picked an enormous skunk cabbage leaf to use as a berry bowl, keeping an eye out for bears.

When she heard a wagon coming, she crouched behind a massive stand of ferns that dripped with morning dew. Her teeth began to chatter. Her head felt light. The berries weren't filling the empty pit in her stomach fast enough. Adelia needed to eat.

As the wagon approached, she heard singing. She wondered if everyone sang songs when they didn't know someone was listening. Unlike the farmer singing to his cows, this woman's voice was high and appealing. Adelia was not afraid of women.

*Sweet violets, sweeter than the roses,*
*Covered all over from head to toe,*
*Covered all over with sweet violets.*

Adelia had never begged before. She supposed if she could learn to steal, she could learn to plead. She stepped out into the road, startling the chunky little mare that pulled a buckboard. The horse snorted, the woman driver yelped, and Adelia spoke. "Morning, ma'am."

"Goodness, child. You gave us a start."

"Yes, ma'am. Sorry, ma'am." Adelia did her best to smile since people seemed to like that sort of thing. Cora Dixon had once said she had dimples whatever that meant. She held up the wide leaf with its load of berries. "Wondered if you might have some other food to trade for these salmonberries. They're nearly ripe."

The woman looked down at her from the high bench seat. "You hungry?"

It was hard to admit. Adelia blushed but forced herself to say, "Yes, ma'am. I am hungry."

"No shame in that." The woman turned on her seat and dug into a basket beside her. "Keep the berries. And here is corn bread. Stale, I'm afraid, but fillin' when you need it."

"It is perfect." Adelia's stomach urged her on as she reached for the large yellow square.

"Now jump in the back of the wagon if you want a ride to Seaside."

Adelia set her food prizes into the flatbed and clambered up.

"My name is Ida Rose. Yours?"

"Adelia," she said when she had gulped down a dry chunk.

"Well, Miss Adelia, don't get crumbs on those blankets. They're for Seaside tourists to handle."

Adelia looked at the folded woolens with their bold native wildlife patterns. She recognized the look, but felt confused by Ida Rose's very fair skin. "You a Clatsop?"

"Nope, but one taught me how to make 'em. I be a used up white woman. Too old and ornery to worry about being on the road alone."

"They are so pretty," Adelia said, wanting to touch one of the blankets but afraid the berry juice on her hands would stick. "Have to be addle-pated not to want one. Seems to me you could sell all you make if some Clatsop and Chinook ladies helped out. I've seen those Seaside tourist before. They buy a lot." It had been so long since Adelia talked with someone who seemed interested. Someone who seemed kind.

"Well ain't you just a Joan Jacob Astor," the woman said with a chuckle. "A couple of them work with me carding the wool, spinning it, knitting it. Then I sell door to door in Seaside or on the street to visitors. Even an ugly white woman like me gets more than Indians moneywise, so I front for them. Nobody needs to know who makes what."

"Takes grit for that, Ida Rose, ma'am."

"Hornswaggling tourists, you mean? Not at all, girl. They go happy, Indians go happy, I go happy. Nobody gets hurt. Giddap, hoss."

The horse plodded, and Adelia ate. The stale bread tasted like heaven.

The sounds around them were of a world going about its morning: the cry of an eagle, wind in the trees, a roar of breakers on the beach far below, the protests of the wagon lurching over ruts. At the top of Tillamook Head, Ida Rose stopped her mare once more. She grabbed up a book, climbed down from her seat, and walked to the cliff. There she stood.

Adelia followed along, coming to a halt beside her, the twelve-year-old not much shorter than this tiny adult. She stared where the woman was staring.

"Know what Mr. William Clark said about this spot? He and Sacagawea and them must have stood right about here." She rifled through pages of the dog-eared book. "Let me see...here. He wrote this view is one of 'the grandest and most pleasing prospects which my eyes ever surveyed...the Seas rageing with emence wave and brakeing with great force from the rocks....'"

Adelia saw just that, along with Tillamook Rock Lighthouse far at sea.

"Ain't that somethin'? And Mr. William Clark went across the country. He seen a thing or two. And now here we are. You and me."

By the time they crested Tillamook Head and the wagon picked up speed down the other side, they both were singing *Sweet Violets*. When they arrived in Seaside, Adelia jumped down, waved a good-bye to Ida Rose, and walked to the beach where she sat in the sand, still humming the song.

She warmed in the mid-morning sun, the sand hot under her butt and legs. She needed rest from her journey. On this side of the Head, she could still pick out the lighthouse and the vastness of the sea beyond. Her father told her there was land over there somewhere, a place called China from whence trader ships came filled with arcane booty. They aimed at the mouth of the Columbia, just to the north of Seaside.

George Wright claimed Terrible Tilly kept them from smashing against the coastal rocks that gave this place the nickname Graveyard of the Pacific. "Two thousand ships went down before the light went up," he'd said to her. She tried to think of her father as a hero.

She rested in the sun while the tide ebbed, enjoying the arguments of seabirds amidst the happier sounds of people on the beach. In time, she stood and scavenged a sturdy stick of driftwood with a hook shape on one end. And as Lilac had taught her, she began to dig for razor clams.

As she worked, she gave a thought to the farmer. He had reminded her of this skill. She saluted him by singing his song, with the proper lyric in its proper place.

*No longer the slave of ambition,*
*I laugh at the world and its shams,*
*As I think of my pleasant condition,*
*Surrounded by acres of clams.*

---

In the rest of *Fog Coast Runaway*, a novel of historical fiction, Adelia works in a hotel scullery, is hunted as a witness to murder of a guest, hides in a logging camp, then moves to Astoria, where brothels abound along with shanghaied sailors and immigrants of every ilk.

*Author Intro*

# TERRY SAGER

From a young age, I was a fan of Alfred Hitchcock, drawn to psychological thrillers and what they revealed about the human mind. My interest continued and I received a B.S. degree in Psychology. My ongoing fascination with exploring the dark side of the human psyche is expressed through my writing. I am a member of the Pacific Northwest Writers' Association and was a finalist in their literary contest.

I volunteer at local animal rescues and am a Small Animal Massage Practitioner. When I'm not writing I enjoy exploring the rugged beauty of the Pacific Northwest with one of my dogs, Cricket.

Terry can be reached at terrysagershuck@gmail.com

## FOR THE GREATER GOOD

Maybe Jim would still be alive if I hadn't gone to the diner for breakfast that morning.

As I left the diner, I passed Sam's cluttered newsstand. It was April 8, 1966, a Friday. Bright red letters on a black background caught my eye. The cover of *Time* asked, "Is God Dead?" I had a better question: *Who the hell cares?* He's sure as crap not going to help *me*. Never has, never will. But the cover gave me pause. I gave Sam thirty-five cents and picked up a copy.

I folded the magazine, stowed it under my arm and continued two blocks up the street to the Clallam County Courthouse. The building and I had recently celebrated our fiftieth birthdays. I stopped for a minute at the bottom of the steps to admire the beauty of it: the architecture, the red brick, the clock tower, its regal presence. This building possessed me. It has not been just my workplace; it has been my place of belonging. Then, as I had done for nearly thirty years, I made my way up the front steps and to my cubby in the Assessor's office.

The rhododendrons would bloom soon, and the trees were wearing the light green of their summer foliage. On this northern coast of Washington, it wouldn't feel like summer until July. This summer I would be able to go fishing any time I want, especially now that Esme was gone. I hated to leave her for too long. Usually, I would go just for the day. Nothing is usual now. Things have changed.

"It's terminal," the doctor said. "You should put your affairs in order."

The county was very kind. Human Resources advised me they were granting me a three month leave of absence.

Not really granted. *Advised. Strongly suggested.* Today was my last workday before the leave started. Maybe, my last workday ever. The doctor's words were so final. No encouragement to fight the good fight. But even if he had tried to give me hope, my body also told me. The twinges of pain in my side were coming more often, and lasted longer. I doubted I would be back. I was past caring.

At lunch, I sat on a bench near the court house and smoked as many cigarettes as my thirty minutes allowed. No need to quit now. I barely remembered the number of tax files I completed that morning but, well, my priorities were different. My mind was elsewhere. And if I'd made mistakes, I guess I'd be forgiven.

I took a mental inventory of my situation. At first, of course, there was denial, but truthfully, as a numbers person, I had to admit I brought this on myself. I had grown a gut from too much gourmet cuisine and too much of the best scotch I could afford. My teeth had yellowed from incessant smoking, just as I had a jaundiced view of life from too much disappointment.

Even so, it would take some time to believe, that soon, I would cease to exist at all. Just a hair past fifty, not really old, but definitely past my prime. *Terminal.* I thought I would greet death with the same resignation with which I usually greeted life. I thought about life too much, felt it too deeply and lived it rarely. I wasn't a father, and only a husband for a brief, hellish time. I had become the office drone I had felt sorrow for, as well as contempt for, in my college days. A spent human being; useless. I always thought I had time for things to change. Maybe even Divine Intervention. At one time, I believed. I hadn't even had a close friend since my thirties, other than Esmerelda, and Jim took *her* from me.

I thought about the cover of *Time* when my brain wasn't occupied with thinking about what Jim had done. I hadn't actually read the article, very unscientific of me, but it got me thinking: *What if?* I never thought God was alive, but I did know Evil was. How about, "Is Evil Dead?" Now that would be an article worth reading. I knew God existed in some people and definitely in animals, but Evil existed too. There was no bearded man in the sky and no red man with a tail and horns living in some fiery pit down below somewhere.

What if, before I was confined to some nursing home, waiting to die, I killed some evil? Maybe, in the time I had left, I had a purpose.

If I kill the evil that God, in his omniscience and his omnipotence has obviously decided to ignore, then I would be acting for the greater good. We all have a bit of evil in us, but we have become experts at keeping it hidden. But, what about the *pure* evil? People who seem to thrive on causing pain. The obvious evil. Could I kill *that*?

Three blocks from home I stopped in front of the General Store. They sold everything imaginable. The window was filled with hand-painted signs, but one caught my attention: "Final Sale! Don't Wait. Over Soon!" I took that as a message meant for me. *Yes, I can kill the cruel and heartless—the ones without a conscience. I can matter. And I mustn't wait.*

As I walked into my little house and threw the keys in the bowl on the table by the door, I remembered it would be Esmeralda's birthday soon. That made me think of Jim again, the bastard.

An hour later, two doors down, I stood on Jim's porch. I heard Walter Cronkite delivering the news—no mistaking the modulated voice, the measured, almost soothing way he reported the horrors of the day. I rang the doorbell and Cronkite went silent. When Jim answered the door, the surprise on his face was expected—we hated each other. But true to his breeding and holier than thou attitude, he invited me in. I counted on that. He led me into the living room, complete with puke green shag carpeting, a citron couch and TV tray sitting in front of it. He tried to be hip, but he too, was too old for that.

I tightened my grip on the gun in my jacket pocket. "So, sorry," I lied. "I've interrupted your dinner." *Hot shot eats TV dinners.*

"It's cool. I was finished. Let me just take this to the kitchen, and I'll be right back. Hey man, have a seat."

This was it. If I was going to matter, I had to do it now. *Don't Wait.* As he headed to the kitchen, I shot him in the back; that particular place on the spine that would paralyze, not kill. Part one. That did the trick. The impact caused the TV tray to fly from his hands. He looked back at me as if trying to understand where the pain was coming from. His body twisted as he went down; he landed on his back. His brain had not fully comprehended what was happening in his perfect world. I knelt beside him, and put one hand on his chest, my other still holding the gun.

As his eyes searched my face, confused, wild fear in his eyes, I said, "This is for Esme. You poisoned her because she peed in your garden. I know it and you know it. She's a cat for God sakes. And now, I see the same fear in your eyes I saw in hers as I sat with her that night, willing her to live.

She didn't survive. You won't either. Good bye, asshole." I shot him between the eyes.

If I hadn't changed my routine and eaten at the diner that morning, I wouldn't have passed by Sam's newsstand, and I wouldn't have seen the cover of *Time*. I would have taken my sabbatical peacefully, knowing I had crafted my own fate and I would have died some night after too much scotch and too many pain pills. I don't know. It must have been Divine Intervention.

One thing I did know was that God *wasn't* dead. I still had a couple good months left. And I had a purpose.

# WAITING FOR YOU

Mia checked her reflection in the empty storefront window next to the restaurant. She wished she were taller and thinner, but she liked the new shade of blonde. Her phone vibrated in her hand. It was Kat: *omw m called some crazy stuff happened.* Translation: Kat would be late, as usual. She'd had another long-winded conversation with her loser boyfriend, Mitchell, so "crazy stuff" could be anything. Mia had commented once that Mitchell and Kat looked like they could be related, with the red hair, blue eyes and all. Kat had laughed. Mitchell hadn't. Mia shook her head and smiled as she tapped *ok* (with a smiley face) and walked into the Urchin.

Connie was usually at the hostess stand, but a Harry Potter clone was there instead. "Bar or restaurant?"

Mia looked up from her phone. "Oh. Hi. I forgot Connie had gone back to school." Connie always put a reserved sign on their usual table during the busy summer months if Mia or Kat texted her ahead of time.

"Yep, Seattle. Bar or restaurant?"

"Uh, bar? There will be two of us. We usually sit over there." Mia pointed to a booth by the window, relieved to see it was empty.

"Cool."

"Cool? Okay, thanks?" Mia shrugged and walked toward the booth. The busy summer season in Port Angeles was over, and the last evening ferry to Victoria, B.C. was leaving soon, so the Sea Urchin was emptying out.

She was unaware "Harry" had followed her until he placed two worn out happy hour menus on the table as she slid into the booth. "Would you like to order now or wait for your friend?"

Mia nearly jumped in her seat. "Oh! Sorry. I didn't know you were behind me. So, you're our waiter, too?" She read his nametag. "Tyler." He looked familiar but she couldn't remember why.

"Not a problem."

Her nerves were frayed after a long day at the art gallery; a steady stream of tourists just buying trinkets. And since Kat was running late, she ordered. "Do you still have that Ediz Hook IPA on tap?"

"Nah. For October it's the Heart O'Hills Pils."

"Someone must've sat up all night to come up with that one, huh?"

Tyler shrugged.

"Okay, then, I'll have that. And would you bring some waters too?" *And get a little personality, cuz you're a little creepy, dude.*

"Got it, Mia. Be right back." Mia wondered how he knew her name and then realized she was still wearing her nametag from work. She took it off and put it in her purse.

The Sea Urchin was their favorite place at the pier to grab a bite and catch up after work. The nautical theme was a bit tired, but during the summer, when it was still light after work, the water view was spectacular. Even now, in the early darkness of October, lights twinkling in the distance gave the place a sense of seaside mystery.

Mia picked up one of the dog-eared menus. With Halloween only two weeks away Mia was surprised the "Ghouls Night" menu wasn't printed yet. It was overused, but still clever. All the usual appetizer names were changed to match the Halloween vibe and there was usually at least one "ghostly" cocktail.

When Tyler returned with her beer, she asked him. "Hey, aren't the Halloween menus out yet?"

Tyler pointed. "Yeah, right there at the end of the table. By the ketchup. Sorry, I'm new, I forgot the bar menus are already on the tables."

He walked away, leaving the old menus. Her eye was drawn to something written in block letters at the bottom of the one she was still holding: WAITING FOR YOU.

People doodled on the menus all the time, but seeing those words, an unsettling chill ran through her. She chalked it up to her overactive imagination and the marketing that went with Halloween. Ads for haunted houses, re-runs of slasher movies and real-life murder mysteries on TV. Halloween-themed *everything*.

Kat arrived, startling Mia as she swooshed into the seat across from her. "Whoa, what's got you so jumpy? Reading Stephen King again? Which one this time, *Happy Hour Horror*?"

"Very funny. That's not one of his titles," Mia smiled sheepishly and took a long drink of her beer.

"Yet. Give him time, give him time. Are you ordering an appetizer?" Kat was turning the menu over and over.

"Wanna split an order of fried calamari? I feel like something fried."

"You look like something fried," Kat teased.

"Well, aren't you the smart ass tonight? Actually, look at this at the bottom of this menu." She pointed out the odd message. "Is there anything written on yours?"

"Nope, not on this one. That's probably left over from a staff meeting or something. Like they were trying to make a play on words: *waiting, serving,* whatever. They have their meetings in here, and someone just needed to jot down an idea. That's all. Not very clever, I'd say."

"You're probably right. Don't know why it struck me as weird."

Tyler took their order and didn't seem nearly as creepy now that Kat had arrived. As he moved to the next booth to take another order, Kat said, "You must've heard there was a break-in at Ethan's place. Maybe that's why you're so spooked."

Mia's eyes widened, "No way. Really? Is that what you meant in your text? Probably just one of his so-called friends from one of his huge parties. You have that many parties with uninvited people and sooner or later someone is gonna lift something. What'd they take?"

"It wasn't really a break-in and it wasn't at *Ethan's* apartment, it was at his apartment *building*. You seriously didn't hear about this?" Kat leaned across the table and lowered her voice. "A girl on the second floor was attacked in her own apartment. I heard she's okay and everything, I mean if you can be okay after something like that—well, at least she's not dead. She either left her door unlocked or someone had a key. They think it was an old boyfriend; that's why you never, ever give a spare key to a boyfriend: rule number 1."

The bartender brought the calamari, a second beer for Mia, a glass of Pinot for Kat. Tyler was evidently already having trouble keeping up with his customers. Mia speared calamari, dipped it in aioli sauce and popped it into her mouth. "The calamari is so good here. Ya know, I had not heard about the attack; that is very disturbing. I mean you can't be too careful who you date and these days you can't be too careful who you break up with. You never really know someone, right? Jeez."

Kat took a sip of her wine. "Yeah. Scary, right? Nothing like a cold glass of wine after a crazy day at work. I think we *both* need to get out more often. It's too long between our girls' nights out."

Mia pointed to the new menus. "You mean "Ghouls Night."

Kat snorted. "You always do that. I almost choked on my wine. But, yeah, we're working too hard, stressing too much, and it sounds like *some* of us are thinking too much!"

"That's true. It's just I get so tired after work that even going out sounds like too much trouble. All I want to do is go home and curl up by the fire."

"And read creepy books that get your imagination all twisted up. I hear ya though. Work can be pretty draining."

They ordered another round and talked about what costumes they were going to wear to Ethan's big Halloween party.

Kat's phone pinged. "Hey, sorry, that's Mitchell. He's at my apartment. I have to catch the next bus home. Let's *promise* to do this again soon!"

Mia rolled her eyes. "Why doesn't he just pick you up? Want me to drive you?"

"He was going to pick me up, but he said his car is in the shop. He's been kind of a douche lately. I'll just catch the bus. It would take you almost an hour to drive me home and back."

"Okay, if you're sure. It was good to catch up even if just for a little while." Mia waved her hand to get Tyler's attention, and he was there as if he had been waiting to be summoned. Kat took notice of the prompt attention. They were both attractive and were used to turning a head or two, but even Kat thought it was a bit weird.

"Thank you," Mia said as he placed the folder holding the bill in front of her. He conspicuously tapped the faux leather top of it as he said, "Have a great night, ladies—it's been a pleasure."

As he walked away, Kat said, "Jeez, he was freaking flirting with you! Did he leave his phone number inside?" Without waiting for an answer, Kat slid out of the booth and grabbed her coat. "Sorry, Mia, but I literally have to run. How much do I owe?"

"Don't worry about it. I got it. Just go. Call me tomorrow." And with that, Kat gave her a mock salute, turned and hurried out of the Urchin.

As Mia opened the folder holding the bill, a piece of paper fluttered out. She caught it before it could fall to the floor. It was typed like a message in a fortune cookie: WAITING FOR YOU.

She felt a chill again, but thought Kat was right, this must be some sort of restaurant promotion teaser, dropping a tag line here and there. It sure got *her* attention. She looked around to ask, but it had gotten very busy and Tyler was nowhere to be seen. She put the piece of paper in her pocket and left enough cash in the folder to cover the bill and the tip. She picked up her jacket and purse and left.

As she took the wind-worn steps to the parking garage underneath the restaurant her mind was filled with horror movie images of parking garages with flickering lights and lots of shadowy places to hide. What better place for a lunatic to be waiting than a parking garage? "Okay, now you're just freaking yourself out. It means nothing. It was just an advertising campaign of some sort—a tease—they're probably working on a new menu or promotion. Chill," she told herself.

The parking garage was actually well lit and although her apprehension faded, she locked the car doors as soon as she got in. She turned the ignition, the car started, and she finally exhaled. She reached home within a few minutes and pulled the car into the driveway of her small house. The living room light was on; it was on a timer. All looked fine. She wanted to change into a pair of yoga pants and a sweatshirt, and watch a good movie; maybe a Disney movie would be a good idea.

Finally settling in on the couch, remote in hand, she remembered she left her cell phone in the car. *Crap, it's starting to rain again.* She grabbed a parka off the coat rack by the door, threw it over her head and hurried out to the car. Within a couple of minutes, she was back in the house, hung up the damp parka, and put the cell phone on the coffee table in front of the couch.

She sat down again, picked up the remote, and began searching *Netflix*. Her cell vibrated, skittering across the glass coffee table. She hit the "read now" button and the message appeared: *waiting for you*. It was coming from Kat's cell phone. "Oh my god. You got me. Really creeped me out this time. Remember though, paybacks are hell, my friend," she said out loud to the message on the screen.

Mia hit Kat's number on speed dial, and within seconds the phone was ringing. The voice that answered was not Kat's.

"Hello," he said.

"Uh, Mitchell? Is Kat there? Let me talk to Kat," she said.

"Kat just ran out to get me some cigarettes. Left her phone..."

*Kat never leaves her phone.* Mia heard the front door creak as it opened—she knew she locked it when she got her cell from the car. She always locked the door. *Always.*

She looked up to see Mitchell with Kat's cell phone to his ear. She'd recognize the pink bejeweled case anywhere. It looked funny in his hand. He continued to talk, eyes locked on Mia who sat frozen on the couch. "Hi, Mia, I've been waiting for you."

Mia's heart hammered in her chest. "What's the joke, Mitchell?"

"No joke. Kat keeps your spare key on her keychain." He walked toward her. "Give me your phone."

"Come on, Mitchell. This isn't funny. Where's Kat?" He ignored the question. "Hey, that Tyler guy was pretty nice, huh? Kind of stupid, but that worked *for* me. The notes were meant for Kat. I told him it was for a romantic rendezvous. He bought it."

Mia swallowed hard. She still couldn't reconcile Mitchell standing in her living room.

"You know Kat's rule. Never give your spare key to you boyfriend? Of course you do. I stole it. And guess whose spare key is on her keyring."

Mia tried to stand up. She'd have to get past Mitchell to get to the front door. She felt like a trapped animal. Then she saw the knife.

Mitchell walked closer and took her phone. "I guess you *girls* should have another rule:  Don't give a spare key to your best friend either."

*Author Intro*

# JOAN ENOCH, MD

I'm "justjoanthegypsy." That's my "handle," because of all the places I've lived in the U.S., the restlessness that has kept me moving, and the "outsider" position that seems to be a basic part of me. My partner, Bob, and I came to the Olympic Peninsula in our mid-seventies to be near family on Bainbridge Island. I'm a retired psychiatrist and psychoanalyst but do occasional consultations on psychological and spiritual matters. I have two sons in their fifties and six grandchildren. My background is New York and Jewish; and I consider myself a Buddhist "wannabe." I'm a lifelong student of consciousness.

I have written poetry on and off, when the spirit moves me, for almost thirty years. I self-published *Shiva Dancing* in the 90s, facilitated poetry and other courses and put together an anthology *Almost Winter* with friends. I hope to publish another book of my poems, *Precarious Positions.* I play poker to relax from ranting a lot about the state of the world.

Joan can be reached at jjthegypsy@gmail.com
She would love to talk about poetry with you.

## NEAR BEACH FOUR

Precipitously perched, the young tree
lives in a precarious position.
The dead, dormant giant beneath
can still give life to the youngster above.
Nourishment is to be found in what remains
alive, but dying by degrees, in the fallen parent.

Why parent, you ask?
A rotting cedar with a Sitka spruce seedling
fallen on its bulky hulk. How can it give life
to a different, but determined youngster?
Parent? Two different species dwelling
together; one felled by age, lightning or man.

The young one taking nourishment  as from a breast
on the body of the other. Later, reaching out, its own root
Trying to find soil but finding only dead tree and air.
The roots form, hug, and hold tight the body of the felled tree.
Moving earthward until they find purchase in the ground
        beneath,
The Sitka then stands tall and straight on the body of the other.

Can we not grow and prosper on and with our earth mother?
Giving back to her and encouraging her to thrive
Can we not share the bounty, generously and gallantly
With all others; loving and respecting all she brings forth
And when we pass, knowing we nurtured the whole world,
Like our dying behemoth cedar nurturing the seed of
        another.

# ORANGE CARPET

based on "Flight Behavior" by B. Kingsolver

While reading Barbara Kingsolver's book
A small segue I took, to write a poem.
She asked a question that's profound
Why so many monarch butterflies abound
In a place they've never been?
An orange carpet of beauty, in a world of sin.
The warming earth is the reason
That they're clumping out of season
On a mountain meadow in Tennessee
Far from their usual Mexican home
Their internal GPS made them roam
To the wrong place, at a time
That's too wet, too cold for them.
And there, they may die, freezing
Perhaps not enough that they're squeezing
Together--no young monarchs in the spring?
A world of loss, for a lost world.


Haiku


Monarch butterflies
Flying everywhere that day
Why so far from home?

## FEBRUARY 2019 SEQUIM

Moving to the big window looking out at the mountains, I watch the heat of the sun work on the snow in the garden, on the cars, and the two-foot berms at the side of the streets. The huge jagged ice chunks clinging to every gutter and overhang, melt and shrink. I wonder, not for the first time, how we can last in a world getting warmer every year.

Icicles weeping
Mourning their diminishment
Lost, as life heats up.

# RANT IN RHYMES AND RHYTHM

I don't have a head that's delightful and dreamy
I don't have a thought that's delicious and creamy
It gets angry and maudlin, melancholic there, too
I often believe it belongs in a zoo
Of pretty unkempt and unusual stuff
That keeps me away from delectable fluff
I don't say this to preen or even to gloat
I write this to you just to keep me afloat
While I promised a poem each week for my group
I'd slip away if I could on a beautiful sloop
I'd loll in a garden of flowers delightful
I'd come to you happy and not a bit spiteful
But I live on a planet heading down a few tubes
With people aplenty and some of them boobs
Who want to destroy the world that we've got
Whose greed and whose worship is money - a lot
Off they go in the world where they hit their own stride
And make us all suffer; this I just can't abide
With too few to buffer destruction and such
All of this makes me want to say much
I can't just say nay to the pain that I've seen
And I really and truly don't want to be mean
But staring so often at the human condition
And with Gaia, our planet, in an awful condition
So before you quit reading my miserable guff
I will quit writing and quietly puff
Up my chest stepping off to the side
Imagining a world we all live in with pride
And I'll thank you all nicely, and brightly and spritely
And hope that the words and prayers we say nightly
Might really make a difference…

## STAY CLOSE

Stay close to your body, was said this morning
As we continued the day's mindfulness practice.
Drifting off to the vastness of mind, I found
The bodies of my poems strewn about
Like ignored, discarded, old rag dolls.
Leaping up, they accused me of favoritism.
We are your body too; the blood, sweat and tears
Of difficult times; the joy of serene moments.
They addressed this to me between the rise
and fall of the breath.
Knowing they were still there, I named them
And let them stay cuddled close
We breathed a sigh of relief, and
Went back to watching our breath.

# WESTERN DREAMS

(written after playing in Ladies Texas Hold 'Em
Championship in Arizona)

The poker room, male sounds, energy, odor
Overwhelmed for a time; two hundred women's voices
Dreaming to reign as Arizona Ladies Champion
A southwestern champion, in that Texas cadillac of poker
With no limits. Tough, desert sharks, these gals
Parse those around them, moving fast, faster
Fastest, in for the kill.

Short stacked, one such dreamer, older than most
Tossed in all her chips. "All in" she cried.
Two  pair against  two ladies tossed cavalierly.
Yes, mine, she breathed at  the turn,  but
She was broken by a third regal queen,
Showing herself at the river.
Beaten. "Old and in the way" she hummed.

Slinking out early, dreams of glory lost, diminished
For the moment, In her view of herself
But hey, that's poker; she comforts herself with that
There's always next year. She heads home; driving
northwest, she's still dreaming, this Brooklyn gal
Western dreams of glory. Still thinking she can be a
"Playa."

## BUDDHA AND PICK UP STICKS

A sitting Buddha
Considers in contemplation
The impermanence of
Meticulously placed
Pick-Up-Sticks

Their solidity seems sacrosanct
Their placement permanent
But the Buddha knows that
Everything arises from cause
And falls away again endlessly.
Standing in the emptiness between
Those artistic renderings
Pondering the teachings of the Buddha
I see myriad possible positions of
Those particular pick-up-sticks.
I "get" in a profound moment
That my forever shifting being
Journeys between birth and death
With no real, immutable
Configuration.
Walking on, I laugh to myself
Wink at this particular Buddha
And enjoy the day
Of art, leisure, and a moment of
Fully conscious awareness

*Author Intro*

# JOHN NORGORD

A Washington native, I was born in Seattle, and graduated from the University of Washington as a mining and industrial engineer. I moved through a number of careers all over the United States before returning to the Pacific Northwest, retiring in Sequim, Washington.

I have extensive experience mountain climbing all over the USA, including the first full winter ascent of Mount Olympus. I served as the second president of the revived University of Washington climbing club and have been an active civic volunteer in each of the several communities I called home, from New Mexico to Sequim.

I completed my first major novel based on a personal story involving the kidnapping of my mother, Alta. It chronicles a twenty-four day forced trip though the west coast and Mexico. I have two other novels in progress that wind through western mining locations interacting with many unique characters and circumstances solving problems that are encountered along the way.

As a new author I enjoy the challenges of bridging the transition from technical engineering writing to more descriptive creative prose.

Contact John at norgordj@olypen.com

## ASCENT OF MOUNT OLYMPUS

I was introduced to mountain climbing in the fall of 1963 when four of my college buddies and I took a course in climbing that was conducted by the Everett branch of the Seattle Mountaineers. The course was based on a book published by the Seattle Mountaineers called *Freedom of the Hills.* All the field activities were great fun and turned us on to climbing glaciers, high mountains, and rock cliffs emphasizing basic skills to avoid or overcome hazards.

In the spring, I joined the University of Washington climbing club. In the fall, after a summer of climbing in the Pacific Northwest I was elected president of the club. I participated in and led many of the club climbs that were mostly attended by inexperienced individuals. There was also a group of very experienced climbers in the club who usually sidestepped the club-planned outings for more challenging adventures such as the first ascent of Mount McKinley's unclimbed west ridge.

Together with my climbing partner, Jan Still, we tackled the Pickett Range and other tough mountain adventures in Washington State. In mid-December of that year a club member, Richard Springate invited us to participate in a winter climb of Mount Olympus. This climb had never been done in the winter. Two very experienced climbers on his team had dropped out at the last minute. John Wells would round out our four-man team.

Springate planned a warm up winter climb of Mount Adams for the following weekend. Loren Steinhauer, a new climbing club member, would replace John Wells who couldn't participate in the warmup. The purpose would be to test gear and tune up for the important year-end exploit.

Springate had already prepared all the food and cooking supplies for both climbs, but we needed good zero-degree gear, snow shoes, ice axes and crampons which both Jan and I already owned.

Setting out on the practice climb on January 11th we arrived at the base of Mount Adams late on a cold Friday. With all other gear loaded in our packs we settled into our tents. Predawn Saturday, tents reloaded, snow shoes attached to our boots, ice axes in hand, we set off for the summit intending to trek the nine to ten miles of 6500 feet of elevation gain up the snow-covered dome. Mount Adams had no glacier hazards such as crevasses or significant uncovered rock outcroppings to avoid so our route was straight up the boring slope. The snow was soft and deep, and our packs contained most of the same gear we would need for Olympus, each pack weighing sixty to seventy pounds including a twelve-pound rock in each to allow for the larger food supply that would be needed for Mount Olympus.

We quickly discovered that under the weight of the added load, even with snow shoes, we sank into the soft new snow which kept us from achieving our normal hiking pace. Loren wasn't in as good a shape as the rest of us and we had to slow down for him.

By five thirty that afternoon when the last shades of day light were fading, we stopped, pitched the tents, and melted snow for cooking dinner and hot beverages. We had intended to reach the summit, but the snow had slowed us down so much that we still lacked three and a half miles and twenty-five hundred feet to gain our objective.

We always organized these trips so we each took turns melting water, preparing meals and pitching the two tents in the evening and prepping breakfast, melting snow plus tearing down the tents in the morning. We decided we could make it to the summit the first thing tomorrow by leaving early in the dark and still get down in time to go home that evening. Since Loren was beat, we let him hit the sack about six p.m. while we washed up and setup for tomorrow's climb. Loren mushed into the sleeping bag like a hibernating bear and was out before 6:30 while the three of us talked for a while.

As a group, this bunch never had the devil far away. Just before we crawled in, we decided to have some fun with Loren. He was scheduled to get up first in the morning and get the stoves and water going. Comfortably inside our sleeping bags we yelled as loud as we could a couple of times, "Loren! We're late, it's time to get up and start breakfast." Loren responding, still in a state of confusion from his almost coma-like sleep, crawled out his sleeping bag, got the four stoves out, fired them up and gathered snow to put in the pots while blurting out, "God, I feel like I hardly slept at all." Each of us laying in the tents were barely holding off the impending guffaws that finally burst out.

He asked, "What's so funny?" In unison we chortled, "Its only seven p.m., you've been asleep half an hour." He responded, "Bastards" and shut off the stoves, then crawled back in his bag. The general kidding deportment for the trips had been set. If we could catch anyone doing anything we considered ungainly or arrogant, we would make the most of it.

We slept like logs awakened by Springate's watch alarm at 5:00 am. The morning of our second climbing day was spent getting closer but not attaining the top. By 10:00 a.m. we could see that we were not going to summit and be down in time to head back to Seattle for school on Monday so after a brief confab we turned tail. The trail back was broken by our previous steps and it had not softened our path with more snow, so we were able to move rapidly and got to the cars as dark overtook us. We were happy with our equipment but recognized from this experience that Mount Olympus, in soft snow, could take five to six days. We would allocate seven.

Three days before we left on the climb, we got together at Springate's apartment and sorted out the food and other supplies. Most of the food was either freeze dried or self-sustaining and  heavy in carbs. Each of us packed our supplies in large thin aluminum boxes called ten-tens. We took the gear and food we were to carry home to put in our pack sacks agreeing to meet on December twenty-eighth in the afternoon and travel to the farthest reachable camp ground on the Hoh River Road in Jan's Nash Rambler. His vehicle had more room than any of our other ones. It also had a luggage rack on top for our gear so all four of us could ride in comfort in a single car.

Loading up at one p.m. that Monday, we boarded the Edmonds Ferry to Kingston and drove three hours to the parking lot at the end of the Hoh River access road. It was dark among the trees and nobody but us was in the End of The Road Campground. We pitched our tents, laid our sleeping bags and gear in them and got ready to arise early in the morrow. We ate a big lunch before we left, so we shared some rolls and cookies, a convenient carb-loaded evening meal.

On Tuesday morning, we finished our cereal with the last of our fresh milk fortified by sweet rolls, then proceeded to stuff our sleeping bags and tents in the packs.

Jan unloaded a one-wheeled device from the car roof he called a deer carrier that he used to transport his kill when he hunted. It had opposing bicycle handlebars at each end connected to a frame built out of three-quarter inch steel welded water pipe. He announced, "We can use this to avoid carrying the heavy packs we have with us."

Since the trail was well maintained and flat for many miles it seemed like a good idea. Hollowed out for animal bodies in its middle, it didn't take much rigging to secure our load. We wouldn't miss the seventy pounds on our backs trekking into the interior. We didn't rationalize that a normal deer weighs one hundred fifty pounds and we were putting two hundred and eighty pounds in the device. It only had propulsion room for two human mules, one in front and one behind, so each pair needed to roll it a mile swapping with the other climbers to rest up

We hit the trail as daylight started poking its way through the trees. This path ran nearly straight next to the wandering Hoh River which periodically looped closer then further away. Wide and graveled, our track ran through the rainforest with many green Douglas fir groves interspersed with massive big leaf maples. The maple branches, devoid of leaves, dark and naked from prolonged rain, were often covered with giant growths of moss that looked like curtains enclosing each tree hanging twenty to thirty feet from the branches. Periodically, we crossed open wet grassy meadows with occasional ponds in them.

Struggling with the transportation device, our walking pace was almost as slow as our Mount Adams uphill warmup adventure. We encountered a significant problem when we came to a narrow one log bridge complete with a one-sided hand rail that crossed a creek running into the river. We almost dumped our deer carrier and its contents into the creek. Shortly after that Wells spoke up and said, "This carrier is slowing us down. It's time for each of us to take up our packs and get going." At that point we had reached the four-mile marker.

We passed a wooden shelter called Five Mile Island. It had four wooden bunks in it and a cedar shake roof with a nice fire pit for cooking in front. I hadn't been in the inner Olympic Forest before and was impressed with the accommodations, figuring if we stayed in these the whole way, we wouldn't need tents.

Just as darkness descended, we gained the second shelter, Olympus Shelter, at nine and a half miles in with the same setup. After hot chocolate and dinner, we retired settling into the warmth of our down sleeping bags that were placed on air mattresses, atop the wooden bunks.

Everybody climbed into bed anxious to sleep so we could continue our imperative early morning start routine. After an hour of snoozing a funny skritching sound woke the three of us, while Springate remained asleep. Directing flashlights toward the noise, we discovered two small spotted skunks had entered the shelter. We had left the top off one ten-ten can and the skunks had gotten into it and pulled out a one-meal plastic bag of breakfast cereal. They were fighting over who was going to get most of their find. I climbed down sending both critters scrambling to the far corner and fetched another bag of cereal so they would both have one. Then getting an agreement from Jan and John I threw the two opened bags under Springate's bunk.

I questioned, "Are we going to wake him up?" In unison we yelled, "Springate!"

He came awake returning a "What?"

"Do you hear that skritching over there, you better look under your bunk."

Retrieving his flashlight, he lowered his head and shined his beam into the eyes of the two little spotted critters no more than two feet away. Pulling his head back quickly he growled, "Jeeze guys, a thing like that could ruin a sleeping bag," which contrasted to the uncontrolled giggles the three of us were broadcasting. Because I had sealed the ten-ten can, the critters had nothing left they could eat, so the varmints finished their snack and left, no spraying occurred.

The next morning, we finished breakfast in the dark, scrubbed up, and were on our way at daylight. After three miles of flat terrain we left the Hoh River starting up a broad canyon to the right, gaining elevation faster than anything we'd experienced to date. Before long we were in our first snow. It was over a foot deep but not fluffy as the elk herd had been traveling the same route. The elk had plowed a packed path through the white mush and left a firm conduit for travel, but the narrow track kept us from using the snow shoes. While we were trudging up the slope, the clouds began to softly rain, firming up our snowy trail even more.

Rain gear on over our down and woolen layers we stayed relatively dry and extended our progress to the Elk Lake shelter by eleven a.m. After a brief lunch, a large snow-covered mountain came into view off to our right. He said, "I think it's Mount Tom."

The further we went the heavier the rainfall became, going from a sprinkle to a drizzle to a steady cold downpour. About three o'clock we bypassed the Glacier Meadows Shelter pushing up another mile and a half to the base of the Blue Glacier. We pitched the tents there and settled in. The rain increased causing us to cook inside the cramped tents. Two hours later, the tents became saturated and began to leak. We packed up everything and spent forty minutes retreating to the Glacier Meadows Shelter where things could remain relatively dry. The weather whims of the Olympic mountains were frustrating to us, but they needed to be dealt with and were a part of our challenge.

Overnight it stopped raining when a cold front moved in and by the morning we awakened to clear skies. We guessed the temperature was in the single digits. The snow on the surface had become saturated well into its depth morphing to a slick, frozen hard, surface. A bad thing? We didn't think so! Keeping our snow shoes mounted on our packs we attached our crampons to our boots and realized our trip up the Blue Glacier had just been given a super boost as we didn't sink in.

Passing last night's preliminary campsite and continuing up the valley, it was hard to tell when we gained the glacier, so we roped up shortly thereafter. Proceeding with caution Jan and I on one rope and Springate and Wells on the other, our progress was slow but steady. The glacier climbed significantly in its lower two-thirds, but the walk was not hazardous, and we encountered no crevasses, all being filled with the recent snow.

On the last part of the trek up the Blue Glacier we encountered a steeper section. We needed to be careful about crevasses in this steep area but never encountered any. We finally reached a broad flat snow covered plain. In front of us a double-wide metal building appeared. Off to the left we spotted several peaks including one on the southwest side looming taller than the rest. Presumably that was the main peak.

Springate explained, "This flat area is called the Snow Dome. This shed has been located for an International-Geo-Physical-Year scientific team to house themselves while they study the blue glacier, the only one on continent that is still growing."

Springate suggested, "We can open up the IGGY shack and stay inside instead of putting up tents." The two other guys immediately concurred, but I was opposed.

I argued, "The facility is locked up indicating the IGGY people do not want the building disturbed. It has a front door and that has been sealed by a three-inch H-beam with two large bolts with big nuts on them rendering the door air tight to the door frame. Let's pitch our tents on the leeward side where the afternoon sun is shining."

All three argued, "We'll be better off inside. We can see bunks through the window."

Springate announced, "I can undo those nuts, I have pliers on one end of the multitool in my pack." I caved in getting their agreement that we would not disturb anything inside, and only use our own provisions and gear. If it started to rain again, we would stay dry. With Springate's tools the door was easily opened.

Inside, the building had a kitchen counter where we could prep meals. Of course, there was no water and the stove did not work as building services had been winterized. I speculated, "I guess they must have traveled up and back in a helicopter which brought up all this gear including the building. They obviously didn't carry anything that large up here on their backs."

Springate piped in, "One of them may have climbed the summit pinnacle five winters ago but it's cheating to be flown all the way up here by a helicopter."

The next morning the day broke cold, but clear and sunny. Leaving the hut about eight a.m. we headed for the big tower, the highest point we could see. The snow on the hill was soft. The climb, too steep for snow shoes, took a couple of hours, us taking turns kicking steps as we slowly ascended. By eleven, we had reached the east side of the large tower which presented a vertical face some five hundred feet high from its base, clear of snow, but icy in several places.

Springate insisted he would go first as leader, unfurling his rope and collection of climbing hardware while I took the belay as he started up the cliff. Slightly overhanging in places the going was slow and required many pitons to anchor the route. Ice on the rock had to be systematically scraped off with his ice axe as he went. By twelve thirty he was only sixty feet up when he slipped and fell twenty feet passing his last piton on the way down. Fortunately, it held when I arrested the fall dangling him below the piton. We heard him scream, "Damn I broke my new pack frame." He started back up, getting to the piton, taking another thirty minutes. With all three of us looking at each other questioningly Wells said, "We'll probably get this climbed by noon next Wednesday."

Taking command, I called out to Springate, "Are you sure this is the right route?"

He called back, "I'm Ok, we have to keep going."

We all looked at each other, certain Springate didn't have the foggiest idea what the route should be.

I called, "Springate come down."

He said, "No, we can't turn back."

We all looked at each other again and knew that we weren't in the right place. I yelled, "Springate come down now! If you don't come down, we're going to tie you off, leave you dangling, and go find the right route."

Grumbling, he said, "Ok" and let me lower him back to the ground. We headed up to the right, around the sloped snow hill, which kept going higher as we advanced, slowly turning more westerly. Plunge stepping several hundred feet higher to a place where the topogaphy flattened off, we found ourselves standing on a snowy mound in front of the summit pinnacle's west side. The summit was less than a hundred feet high on this side and had a gentle west face.

This area was gorgeous with several other pinnacles surrounding it and miles and miles of visible snow-laden peaks in the distance surrounding us. The final climb was covered with a three-foot thickness of ice crystals lining a depression in the middle of its face. The obvious route provided a simple path to the top. Springate roped up and John Wells took the belay.

I went across to a gentle snow-covered secondary mound that was just a little lower than the main summit where the view of what existed on this magnificent panorama was spectacular, yielding several excellent photos.

Springate climbed setting one ice screw in the depression and two on the top for repelling. Twilight was coming on and light was leaving rapidly. He was back down in twenty minutes.

Wells said, "John as president of the climbing club you should go second." It took me ten minutes to get on top kicking a few extra steps, my feet crushing the frozen wall material as each step sank into the porous ice crystal makeup of the route's surfaces. My excitement to be part of such a historic climbing event and the unparalleled scenic wonder of the winter scene made my heart soar. I wanted to spend more time on top because it was so beautiful, a mind-blowing experience that I wanted to prolong, but I knew others were waiting below and light was fading fast. Spending a minute on top, I clipped into the two repel ropes descending as fast as I could.

By then we were in deep twilight and visibility wasn't good. Ready to help my two remaining companions summit with flashlight assist I said, "Whoever's next should get going." All three mates responded, "It's too late. We need to get back to camp and not get stranded up here."

We pulled down the ropes, picked up our gear and headed for the IGGY hut, two of our crew swallowing the disappointment of not making the summit, both pissed at Springate for misdirecting our beginning effort.

The next morning, we put the metal nuts back on the door, closed it tightly, and started back down the glacier. We all agreed that the crevasses were full of snow and didn't present a hazard, so we didn't rope up. Springate as usual was leading.

As we crossed over the brow of the snow dome and started down the short steep part, Springate suddenly began sinking into the snow penetrating all the way to his armpits. He spread his arms to stop his disappearing body. We roped up and belayed me as I edged out to rescue him from the hole he had found. When I approached, he warned, "My legs are hanging in a void."

So much for no crevasses. We stayed roped up until we were off the glacier reaching the valley where the elk had been. Springate was irritated that we had laughed at him in his predicament and I didn't blame him, but as team leader he was the first to proclaim our mistaken, "We don't need to rope up."

As we hiked the rain started again and our packsacks took on a few pounds of water. I caught myself thinking, I've carried these snow shoes on my pack the whole trip and we've never used them. We were covering two miles an hour now and going splendidly. When resting a moment, we sorted out who would retrieve the empty fifty-pound deer carrier and roll it back to the car. Springate and I would take it the first two miles and Jan and John Wells the last two.

At the cairn marker, Springate and I picked up the empty device and trudged ahead across the bridge and on for two miles. Darkness had arrived requiring flashlights for this last four miles. We had gotten a little ahead of Jan and John Wells when we dropped the carrier off for them. We heard Wells from a few hundred yards behind yelling "Eat Crap." We thought he was upset that he had to fool with the deer carrier. When we reached the car, we were astounded that we had completed the return trip in one day and would be headed home.

Jan and John Wells showed up five minutes later deer carrier in hand. John questioned, "Why didn't you come back when I called?"

Springate answered, "Why would we when you were yelling eat crap at us?"

Wells responded, "I was yelling heat cramp."

We both went, "Whoops."

Jan announced, "My feet are damaged." As he sat and lifted his feet, we pulled off his leather hiking boots which apparently hadn't provided enough protection from the cold. We discovered he had frozen his entire right big toe and a little of the next toe and three quarters of his left big toe. The right toe and the outside part of the left toe looked like giant blood blisters. All we could do was pad them carefully with extra socks.

I drove his car back to give him as much comfort as I could although he said his toes were numb and didn't hurt too much. Hungry from days of eating freeze dried food we stopped at a road side cafe called Dupuis just short of Sequim on highway 101, where the sign said All-You-Can-Eat Spaghetti and Crab. The place was almost empty, but we ate enough crab and spaghetti for the owners to think they had a full house, acting like typical mountaineers who have been camping in the wild for several days and come across a gourmet meal. We caught the nine something ferry to Edmonds, and everybody picked up their cars which were parked at my Edmonds house.

My wife Gretchen was glad to see me when we arrived and after the three others left, we both celebrated my success with a glass of wine. Jan headed for the emergency room where they bandaged his feet and set up an appointment with a specialist in frozen body parts in Tacoma the following morning. He didn't lose any toes, but he had trouble with his feet for a long time after our adventure.

The psyche of climbers has interesting contrasts. There is a competition among them that says I was the first to do this whether it be a first summit, a new route, or climbing something with the least amount of mechanical aid, for example, no pitons, ice screws, rock bolts. For the real fanatic no ropes, harnesses, or safety equipment, a totally free climb is the ultimate challenge. Others climb to experience the views, the scenery, including the flora and fauna.

"I almost summited" is a big putdown for most, even though you have completed ninety five percent of the trip quitting when it becomes too dangerous to continue.

Leaving gear on the route because it is too difficult to retrieve is also frowned upon and if you can retrieve the remains from someone else's faulty endeavor it gives you plus points saying I'm better than they were.

Many climbers like the mental challenge of scoping out a route especially a new one where you gain climbing societal esteem. Avoiding or mounting a well-known high angle crack, a slick slab or an over-hanging protrusion with a tricky climbing move is immensely satisfying to the died-in-the-wool rock climber.

Might it be better however, if we could forget the competition and just go out and enjoy our time in the wilderness? The book, *Freedom of The Hills* title states the objective most climbers are really after. We can go where we want, see what we can see, and experience what we want to experience, overcoming the challenges with our skill and knowledge.

*Author Intro*

# VIRGINIA TIMM

I received my B.A. from Cal State Hayward in 1966, with a major in English and a minor in speech. In 1967 I took a fifth year of studies at Hayward to earn a secondary teaching credential and moved across the San Francisco Bay to Notre Dame College to earn an elementary certificate while teaching full time in East Palo Alto. I taught third grade students in Indiana and then head start kindergarten children. My own children kept me at home for the next few years. I taught both middle and high school students in the Stockton Unified School District for seventeen years.

In 1986 we moved to Stockton, California and I was able to participate in Saturday sessions of the Area 3 National Writing Project at U.C. Davis. During the summer of 1994, I became a fellow of the Area 3 writing project. Our motto for our summer t-shirts became "I Search, I Write, I Am." That was our daily endeavor.

Although I don't write that often now, I am grateful for the opportunities for writing offered at the Sequim Library on the third Monday of each month.

I am currently working on a children's book with a Christmas theme.

Contact Virginia at vmt63044@gmail.com

# WALKING WITH HELP

Difficult it is, to hold steady on uneven ground for the very young
and the very old.
Grandma slipped her hand around mine, held tight,
        so that I would not fall.
She foretold a time when I would be the one
With strong arms, sure feet, and a steady pace.

Such a time was beyond my young comprehension.
That time too soon came.
I became the giver,
She the unsteady one.
I looped my arm around hers,
Held close as we descended the tilted, jumbled stairs,
Leading to the road in front of my house.
As she had predicted, life had almost played her out.
She needed me as I had needed her.

My granddaughter shakes free from my grasp,
Races ahead, only occasionally, tauntingly, glances back.
Then takes my hand to steady me over the uneven ground.

*Author Intro*

# GORDON ANDERSON

In the early 1970s, I began writing on a weekly basis, and once retired I began writing almost daily. Before twenty, I wrote on napkins and scratch paper at times but life got in the way—with part-time and full-time hell-raising, hard physical work at many jobs and the seeking of higher education. I schooled on-and-off, part-time and full-time for thirteen years. I earned my degree from SDSU.

My wife and I moved to the Olympic Peninsula in 1997 and we live in Port Angeles. I retired in 2002 from the US Postal Service.

My six books include three volumes of *Gordito Haiku,* each containing 300 Haiku and 60 Tanka poems; *Looking Through the Knothole,* is a book of 100 Tritina poems; *Chosen Poems: Words of Love* is a book of love poems; *Morning Coffee* is a book of 126 Free Verse Poems. My seventh book, *Porch Poetry* is a book of 162 Rhyme and Lyric Poems to be published this year.

My paperbacks and E-books are sold on Amazon and through my website.

Gordon can be reached at www.echospringspub.com, or by email at either echospringspub@gmail.com or dreamsandthoughtsga@gmail.com.

# SIX HAIKU

Hurricane Ridge
white, pink, blue and indigo
—June flowers are out

In green grass meadows
down below Sol Duc Hot Springs
graze Roosevelt Elk

Staircase Waterfalls
from Hoh forest to the sea
—endless water flows

A mirror image
a Dungeness reflection
—the river shimmers

Harpooning a whale
the meat will be shared by all
—Makah celebrate

From a driftwood log
at high tide three crows stand still
today at La Push

# MOUNTAIN GHOSTS

I leave the winding road
with an early morning sun
to hike the long trail
to reach the waiting cabin
below the tall white mountains
before the day is done

I pass deer in the woodland fields
and walk under eagles in the sky
to reach the river's bank
and the waterfall nearby
where I see a beautiful rainbow
and I feel so gratified

From there I continue on my way
to cross a weathered plank board bridge
that opened into a green grass meadow
below a curving golden granite ridge
where I step into a tall tree forest
and Mother Nature makes me feel rich

And in short time I reach the log cabin
my intended weekend journey's goal
I sit down on the old wooden porch
and there I make my happy toast
to my very lucky outdoor life
and to all my ancestors' mountain ghosts.

## DOUBLE LOOK FROM EDIZ HOOK

At the east end
out by the Coast Guard Station
one can get a—double look
from Ediz Hook
to the north across the strait
not too far-off
 is land—Victoria B.C.
—where I've sipped English tea
 with some Canadian friends

In any year and most any season
one can get a—double look
at rain and wind
or waves and fog
—and the coming and going
of currents and tides
plus boats and ships
from out on the hook

At the east end
out by the Coast Guard Station
one can get a—double look
from Ediz Hook
to the south off in the distance
above my home—the mighty Olympics
with their white caps show
beyond the winding road
up to Hurricane Ridge

In any year most any season
one can get a—double look
at birds that fly
and birds that nest
at fishermen or the Blackball Ferry
—and from time to time
see feeding whales
from out on the hook

At the east end
out by the Coast Guard Station
one can get a—double look
from Ediz Hook
and see the deep blue
Port Angeles town harbor
where I live below the high mountains
and the place I want to be

Today—I am out on the hook
feeling a cool sea breeze
and smelling the salt in the air
I am once again—getting my
double look from Ediz Hook
standing on the Strait of Juan de Fuca.

# COULD WE JUST TALK

Could we just be—you and me?
no middle man—no in-betweens
could it just be—you and me
no touch tab screens—no e-machines

Could we just talk—and maybe walk?
one on one—before we're done
share some fun—attention
could we just talk?

Please—hear my plea—you and me
no plugged in schemes—no high tech themes
no lap top needs—no e-mail feats
no text to read—no message tweets

Could we just talk—and maybe walk?
one on one—before we're done
share some fun—attention
could we just talk?

No lap top needs—no e-mail feats
no text to read—no message tweets

Could we just talk—and maybe walk?
one on one before we are done
share some fun—attention
could we just talk?

# AMERICAN LIKE ME

This American was talking—
now let me see—you don't think like me
you're different—you're unstable—you're unable
I guess—you don't have a clue—maybe you're cuckoo

This American kept on talking—
you're idiotic—unpatriotic
surely different—maybe even sick—a lunatic
now—I've got to set you straight—before it's too late

Don't you see —you don't have the same friends that I do
your views are not my views with not the same taboos
—our politics aren't the same—I can't pronounce your name
—you're not an American like me
your race—religion and creed is something I don't need
don't you see you're not like me
—you're not an American like me

This American kept on talking—
so—shame on you—you don't think like me
you're different—you're full of bull—you're a radical
you're maybe off your rocker—maybe gone bonkers

This American kept on talking—
and you do not reside—where I do
we are not the same—you are not like me—you're different
you are not a real American like me

Can't you see —you're not an American like me
you don't think or talk like me—
you don't act or dress like me
you don't play my social games—
you don't have my same aims
—you're not an American like me
your world is not my world—you're not my boy or girl
don't you see you're not like me
—you're not an American like me

You'll never be an American like me
you're of lower class—our social lives don't match
there's just too much contrast–you don't stand a chance
there is just no way you'll ever be
—an American like me.

# TIDE POOL SMILES

The sea waves crash
the sea foams splash
I'm on the beach
again at last
I'm waiting for the tide to slack
and wash out and then come back

It's tide pool time
between the rocks
to look into pools
and watch the clock
to see what I can hopefully see
like starfish and anemones

My time is short
down on my knees
seeing little fish
and green seaweeds
when I realize big waves grow
and tides come back—it's time to go

To be safe again
upon the beach
to wait the low tide
out of reach
then it's back to intertidal shore
where I can grasp and study more
among the jeweled pools awhile
where I can wear my tide pool smile.

*Author Intro*

# RUTH GEIGER

My life has been filled with many joyful experiences and too many obstacles.

My present joys include: my wife Brenda- we begin and end each day with "Good morning/ night I love you!," my supportive sister Eileen, my wonderful daughter Magalie, my energetic grandchildren, traveling and meeting wonderful people, weeding our acre plus, studying Spanish (I'm terrible at it, but I love to study), writing, and loving friends.

Past joyful memories include: working as a correspondence teacher in Alaska, working as a blue collar worker in Minnesota, attending seminary in Texas, pastoring churches in Seattle and Alaska.

Obstacles Include: a dysfunctional birth family, a divorce from my husband, five difficult adopted children (four from Haiti and one from the US), saying goodbye to our faithful Golden Retriever, Sadie.

Presently I am working on a book called *Poems with an Edge.* and plan to publish this year. I have three other books in progress: *Reflections on Life, Memoirs,* and *When Love Isn't Enough: Parenting a Mentally Ill Child.*

Contact Ruth at ruthgeiger@olypen.com

## WAVES OF GRIEF

Once I liked to body surf.
Not today.
Prior pleasure diminished.
waves of sadness
wash over me.
The tide pulls me
into deeper water.
Taste the salty water.

Waves push me
first one direction,
then another.
My feet
more wisdom than my head
search
for a stable place to stand.
There is none.
Only the precarious sand.

Current comes in
drags me to the shore.
I cannot get up.
I don't want to get up.
Brief thoughts
interrupted by breaking waves.
Deposited again
in waves of sadness.

Waves
take me where they will.
They pull me back
as I remember
our time together.
My best friend.
Gone from this life.

In the sound of crashing waves
I hear her voice.
Bossy as usual,
she tells me what to do.
As usual, I resist.

She tells me where to swim.
I don't want to swim anymore.
My tears become foam on the sea.

Her spirit calls me again.
This time using logic,
"Come out of the water
You will drown."
I remind her
even sand is unstable.
I will remain here
splashing in waves of grief.

She says, "I love you.
Come.
We will walk together on the beach."
"For how long?" I ask.
"For as long as you need."
Cold waves splash my feet.

We walk together.

One day
I will say goodbye to these tears.
We will embrace and
my spirit will join her spirit.

But not today.

## DRESSER DRAWER BABY

Right from the hospital
into my arms
a new mother
a new baby.

My first adopted child.
We wait
in a Philadelphia hotel
unsure, scared, delighted.
A myriad of emotions
no one to guide us.

She cries.
Do I feed her?
Burp her?
Change her?

How do I feed her?
With breasts to suck
but no milk inside.
A bottle instead.

Feed her
Burp her
Change her

A leaky, crooked diaper
doesn't work.
Try again
Success.

What's next?
A bath
for a newborn?
Only six pounds
thirteen days old
smaller than a cabbage patch doll.

She needs sleep
but where?
A crib?
Too big
My bed?
Too dangerous.

Search for a solution
I see it.
A dresser drawer
filled with soft things
blankets and more
all infused with my love.

Into the dresser drawer.
The drawer into the crib.

She sleeps.
I watch.
I ponder.
Will she be as safe as this
when she grows up?
Probably not.

Silence broken
she cries.
I rock her
we rock together
Her tears become my tears.

Some day she will move
beyond this drawer
out of the crib
into her own path.

Moments of joy.
Moments of challenge.
Moments of heartbreak.

Until then
rest my precious one
my dresser drawer baby.

# CONTROLLED BY LISTS

My life.  Controlled by lists

- To do list

- Christmas list

- Grocery list

- Laundry list

- Packing list

My Problem?  Can't find my lists.

## BREAKFAST

I wanted a soft boiled egg
Got out the pan
Filled it with water
Turned on the burner
The phone rang
Talked for awhile
Time for breakfast
Never put in the egg
No Breakfast
Still hungry

# A LITTLE CRAB

Wide as he is tall
Beady eyes on top.
How far can a crab see?
Can he see me watching him?

He runs to the waves
Runs back again
Cannot make up his mind.

There are risks in the ocean.
Seals, fish
Other crabs.

There are risks on the sand.
Hungry birds.
Crabby people.

From the sea
To the sand.
From the sand
To the water.

Gymnastics on the waves
Tossed to the beach
He pulls inward.
Curls into a ball
Unwilling to risk again.

When uncertain
We too pull inward.
Just like the little crab.
Unsure which way to go.

Life will decide
If we don't.

# DEATH

Death
No breath
No Life
Ends our past
Robs our future
No
Releases the past
Opens the future

*Author Intro*

# ELIZABETH K. PRATT

I've adopted the town of Port Angeles as home since 2005, after moving from Oregon. Since I can tell a pine from a fir from a hemlock, I'm allowed to stay. My day job is working with elders seeking assistance, and my hobby is helping children learn to play music on stringed instruments. In the in-betweens, I can be found exploring and photographing the great Northwest on foot, bike or kayak, or just relaxing at home with my five rescue cats. The vegetable garden in my back yard is my science lab (did you know red-skinned potatoes bloom purple?). When all work is done, I love a good story, well told, and learning to play new music with the Sequim Community Orchestra.

You can find my writing in *Compass & Clock* magazine, the flash-fiction anthology *Itty Bitty Writing Space*, and previous editions of *In the Words Of Olympic Peninsula Authors*.

Look for Beth's photography of nature and cats alike on Instagram or Facebook. Contact her at beth132pratt@gmail.com

# GAME ON!

Their silver whistles gleamed by fluorescent tube light, casting bright reflections on the gloss-polished concrete floor. They walked in triangular formation, all six mindful of their status within the pack. Across the back of the spearhead, the special needs teacher took center position with the cheerleading and girls' volleyball coaches at the corners. The three pillars of machismo took the fore: football coach Ferrell, flanked by the baseball and basketball coaches, always took the point.

The men sported bushy moustaches but were clean cheeked, their hair buzzed with military precision. The women of the rear guard wore matching pony tails, their big bangs bouncing in hair sprayed uniformity against scowling brows.

Each coach carried a red or blue rubber ball, the same as used in kickball every spring. But this was mid-winter. It could mean only one thing.

Coach Ferrell halted the parade between the fifth and sixth grade lunch tables, where a fearful hush befell the smallest students. Some froze in place, sandwiches and fish sticks held at half-mast.

The coach chomped audibly on his wad of pink Hubba Bubba, letting fear spread through the herd before he spoke. "Let's head for the gym, kiddos. Time for a tournament. We'll take fourth and sixth grades with us." He gestured with his red ball to his left and right. "Fifth and seventh, you're with them," and he nodded over his shoulder. On cue, the women raised their balls in salute. "Sudden death. Last man standing wins for his team. Any questions?"

Jimmy Wilcox, new that week from a school in Chicago, raised a hand, apparently oblivious to the terrified stillness of his fellow fourth grade classmates. "Coach? What kind of tournament?"

Stalking forward like a panther on the prowl, Coach Ferrell fixed his sights on the small city boy. For Ferrell, football was king, and the tournament was a drill with one goal: eliminate the weak. These matches determined the future athletic fate of these flimsy children. Who would be water-boy and who would be quarterback?

Looming before Jimmy, his polyester jersey and shorts blazing in bright white and cobalt blue, he bounced the red ball in one short pop from the top of the boy's carefully gel-spiked head. "Jimmy, the game is dodge ball. And, son, you are already out."

# MANDY

Mandy stepped carefully across the paddock, dodging piles of dung and puddles where hooves had scraped holes in the hard-packed earth. She slipped between the fence rails when Mother went into the kitchen to get her coat from the back of Daddy's chair.

"Mandy, stay here and wait for me," Mother had said before leaving the child sitting in the tall grass. But why should she wait? The horses were her friends. She didn't need Mother to visit Daisy and Buck.

She heard the slam of the rickety screen door before Mother's voice rang out across the yard, "Mandy! Girl, where are you?" Soundless, Mandy scurried to the wide-open barn door and ran across the hay-strewn floor.

Mother's voice always seemed quieter when Mandy was inside the barn. The sound was muffled behind the blowing and snorting of the horses, the scratching of the hens, the mewling of the barn cat's new litter of kittens hidden in the pile of worn saddle blankets. The light of the falling evening filtered between the rough planks of the west wall.

"Hey, Daisy," Mandy said, stretching up to rub the velvet nose of her favorite friend on the farm.

"Mandy! You better not be alone in that barn!" Mother's voice boomed as she came in through the tack room door.

Mandy ducked into Daisy's stall and crouched low, out of sight. She heard the jangle of metal when Mother brushed past the bridles hanging from their pegs.

"Damn it, Mandy!" Mother barked. "It's gonna be hell to pay when I catch you! I'm gonna tan your hide if you don't come out this minute!"

Mandy looked up into Daisy's big, soft eyes and held a finger to her lips, shook her head. "Quiet!" She barely breathed.

Daisy bobbed her head and nickered. Buck, in the next stall, whinnied back and stamped a heavy hoof.

"I'm telling you, girl," Mother yelled as she slammed the stall door wide, sending it banging against the wall from which the hinges hung askew.

The big mare's eyes rolled, white flashing bright in the dimming light, and she reared back on her haunches, pawing at the air before crashing down to the dirt floor.

Mandy didn't make a sound when the sharp shod hoof smashed into her frail skull. The only sounds were a short, soft exhale and the gentle thud of her tiny body falling sideways into alfalfa scraps littering the stall floor.

# GOING HOME

The three-hour drive would have taken her to the empty rental leased a week before. The hollow, alien house that was her new adventure, her new place alone. Not the home they had shared in love, in lonely apathy, in angry argument, in making up again.

But she didn't drive to her new home.

She ignored the gleaming white arrow pointing toward her winding, shadowed road. Instead, she turned up the stereo and sped the long wide straight of Interstate 5.

She should have been home hours ago, her bags unpacked, and laundry sorted into separating bins, the windows opened to the evening breeze sweeping off the sea. But she was hours away.

Cities and towns, rest stops and casinos, unread mile markers, unfamiliar places, they were a blur unnoticed. A big city skyline loomed as sunset fell beside her, towers of steel and stone and glass bathed in the rose-gold light. The offramps leading away were mysteries left unsolved.

She should have been home hours ago, but the border grew nearer as her past drifted farther behind. A border she could not cross. She slowed and turned at the last option, one leading to nowhere in particular.

A yellow glow of sodium lights greeted her as she pulled into a slot. Hot pink neon letters glared "OPEN" in the window of the greasy spoon. With bleary-eyed focus, she walked toward the door, leaving the car behind, engine still and keys dangling from her weak fingers. The keys that should take her home.

She should have been home hours ago. That home, where her life was new, could wait. The door pushed open before her and she stepped inside.

## IT'S IN THE BAG

I was going to save the world.

All of my eighteen-year-old energy for altruism turned into a focused high-beam, reaching across Broadway and locking onto a young homeless man. Maybe, saving the world would start with him.

Tall, lanky, dishwater blonde, he appeared to be about my age. Leaning against the Pioneer Courthouse fence, he was surrounded by the nomadic men who made up Portland's summertime homeless population of the 1990s. They wore weary expressions and denim so dirty that it was no longer blue. The young man had a cleanliness and energy that revealed his newness to the life.

Shoulders squared, my approximation of a dazzling smile cemented in place, I strolled across the street, the pavement a wavy illusion in the August sun, and approached him. "How are you today?"

He didn't reply immediately. Slow surprise spread across his features as he realized I was speaking to him. "Oh, uh, hi, ma'am, I'm just fine. How 'bout yourself?"

My lip curled at being ma'amed. "I'm Judy, what's your name?" I pushed my smile out, through the grimace.

"Michael. My friends call me Mike." He slouched against the fence. His companion, a grizzled middle-aged man with two big mutt-dogs on frayed ropes, did not react to my presence.

"Mike, I am so happy to meet you! Do you live in Portland?" I locked my gaze into his. "Do you go to school?"

"Oh, ma'am, I'm traveling now, no more schoolin' for this guy. I'm seein' the world."

With sudden interest, his dog-owning friend turned toward us and smiled with pride in his beloved protégé. He slung an arm loosely over Mike's shoulders, "I take care of this buck, young lady. What business is it of yours?" His eyes were cold steel.

"I work down at Trend College. We're enrolling for GED and college prep courses for the fall. Mike, have you considered going back to school?"

Steel Eyes answered instead. "This boy will get all the learnin' he will ever need, on the road, little miss."

"Mike, I can help you here, help get you an education. We have resources, can help you find housing, maybe even a job." I refused to let Steel Eyes dominate this conversation, even turned to try and cut him out. Mike was my project now. I would save him. It did not occur to me that my idea of "saving" might not be at all appealing to Mike.

Steel Eyes was soon distracted, though, by a new arrival at the fence. The new arrival was weaving, eyes at half-mast, a stink of cheap wine and old sweat wafting from him. His bronze skin was stretched tight and shiny across his broad, grinning face. In his hands, he clutched a crushed brown bag around a bottle hidden inside. Swaying and tilting on his feet, he seemed very close to collapse. Steel Eyes helped him to the ground, settling him next to one of the dogs.

Mike didn't answer my question. He bent to pet the dog closest to the drunken man, who continued to swig from his brown bag. "Ol Chief here, he's seen more than any man I know." Mike looked up at me, "Wanna pet him?"

The summer heat cooked the smells of the city into a unified aroma, blending almost-melting asphalt, perspiring humans, hot garbage, and urine. The smell of unwashed dogs was a minor component.

I let Chief sniff my hand and patted his head between floppy brown ears. "Seems like a nice dog." Maybe I could get him to refocus on my questions if I could find some common ground. "Do you have a dog of your own?"

Mike reached down into the heap of Army-green knapsacks, bedrolls, and rags. When he straightened, he held a remarkably clean, bright purple and gold Crown Royal bag by the drawstrings. Gently cradling the bag in his dirty palms, he loosened the string, reached in, and pulled out a pink-nosed, white and grey rat. The bag squirmed as he re-tied the string. That rat was not alone.

"This is Candy. Cane and Arnie are still inside. Want to hold him?" His eyes sparkled. He stroked the rat, let it climb to his shoulder.

It took a huge effort not to step backward. "No, thank you, Mike."

He laughed. "Pretty girls like you never like rats. But they're good pets. Loyal. These three never let me down."

Mike took Candy from his shoulder and loosened the strings on the bag again. He moved to slip Candy back inside, but the gods of chaos had other plans.

Chief and his dog-friend both lunged at Candy, who squeaked and leapt to the ground. Mike scrambled to catch the escaping rat, who was now skittering along the fence, looking for refuge from the barking and snarling. As the dogs strained against their ropes, they tangled around the drunken man, tipping him to his side. The paper bag hit the ground with a muffled sound of shattering glass, shards breaking through and cutting into his hands.

Steel Eyes hollered, "Mike! Get that critter and help me!"

My feet felt cemented in place. I was watching, wide eyed and breathless, through an invisible screen, one I could not step through.

Mike caught Candy and stuffed him into the purple felt bag. Steel Eyes gathered his own pile of belongings. The drunk man was now unconscious, still grinning, curled up in a pool of cheap red wine and blood from his sliced palms.

"Hurry, before the cops show up!"

Both Steel Eyes and Mike had their packs on their backs, dogs tied to their belts. The men further down the fence watched, detached but curious; they did not join in the frenzy.

"Get an arm around him!"

Mike hoisted the unconscious drunk to his feet but could not juggle his belongings and balance the man. "Take this!" he shoved something into my hands. "I'll be back!"

I stood rooted to the ground, as Mike, Steel Eyes, the drunk man, and two dogs, encumbered by all their bulky possessions, disappeared into the growing rush hour crowd.

Almost all their possessions.

The thing I held in my hand moved.

Mike had given me his precious bag of rats.

I waited for a while, watching for them to return along the path that had been their escape route. The bag, now dangling from my fist, wiggled and squirmed. It was after 4:30, and I needed to go back to the office.

One more futile look up and down the street, hoping to see Mike's lanky frame striding back up the sidewalk, but he did not appear.

I hung the bag by its golden string on a fence post, right where Mike had leaned. "He'll be back," I whispered to the squirming trio before I turned and walked away.

*Author Intro*

# VYKKI MORRISON

I am a Port Angeles resident with a passion for writing and art. Growing up surrounded by the magic of the Vermont hills, I found my muse early, and have been writing since the age of eight. Over the years I've moved around a bit, but in 2015 the lure of Washington called. My muse responded, finding joy and a home in the beautiful Washington countryside.

Vykki says her writing can be found in a number of venues in the States and Canada, including some very old refrigerator doors.

Contact Vykki at veryvyk@yahoo.com

# GOD AND MOTHER NATURE

Mother Nature lost the bet. It was a good hand, but not good enough to beat God's, who was omniscient and could read her cards. By that time, however, she was too drunk to remember, so now she was paying the price.

Behind her, angels tittered. Mother Nature whirled round, stepped on her mossy-green gown, and toppled over the edge of the platform onto a newly formed planet.

She landed hard, creating what would one day be called the Grand Canyon by its residents, although it didn't feel so grand to her. Wiping dust from her posterior, she unsteadily rose and returned to her earlier position. With a flick of her fingers, the angels who laughed at her morphed into a celestial choir of stars.

God grinned. He knew He had her, and secretly He really enjoyed watching her work. If only she wasn't always tipsy. He sighed.

"Look," He said, "it's almost the weekend, and I'm due for a nap. I've already updated the forms. The planet is yours. All you need to do is put my plan into action.

I've already made the heaven and earth, complete with lighting, and," He frowned, "that dent you just made. You've spilled your mead all over the place, you've made my work muddy and filthy, *and* you've lost the best two out of three.

So no more stalling. Go to it. We need wholesome, creative effort, a little splash of color, some of the genius only you have. But we want *this* one to work, so have some coffee. You've already botched three of my planets."

Mom gave a little hiccup, and smirked, thinking of the seven-legged fritterleys on that first frozen planet, doomed to honk at the frequently increasing group of stars she created, twikkoving and plushing. Or was that twinkling and pulsing? And really, who cared?

The problem with God as she saw it was that He liked to make His universes structured and orderly. Boring. She, on the other hand, was all about creative license.

Looking down, she noticed her chalice was empty. "Hit me fellas," she shouted sloppily to the mead-pouring cherubim hovering over her. "And another one for my friend, too."

Pretty Lucifer peeked out from behind God, waiting to see what came next. Slowly, unsteadily, Mother Nature drew herself up to full height. She attempted to snap uncooperative fingers, and God, way ahead of her, grabbed for the mead bottle. Mother Nature also made a grab, and suddenly, like a cloth pulled from a table by a magician, they found themselves falling onto nothingness.

"Oh, crabapples," Mother Nature muttered, sitting up.

She saw the platform that had been under their feet and pulled it to her. Forming it into a ball, she lobbed it at the stars, who were valiantly attempting to reform into angels. She grinned, her good spirits restored.

God, who found Himself lying on a vast field of nothingness, roared His displeasure.

"Finish that planet, and you'd better do it right this time, or *else*, you...you...lush—You..." Words escaped Him. Frowning, He turned to see Lucifer rolling on the void, laughing crazily. Other angels chuckled to see God, Himself, at a loss for words. He reached out and tossed them over the edge of nothing.

It was only at that point that He realized He might have been a little too extreme. Mother Nature drunkenly gave

Him *the look*, withering and contemptuous. "Now look what you've done," she grumbled. "Those were perfectly good angels, and besides," she gathered steam as the realization hit her, "*they had my mead!*"

Mother worked fast, blowing the newly formed planet under the falling angels. Mead landed with a splash, running into the crevices created during her unfortunate fall, anointing the dust.

A few of the falling angels landed in somewhat unfortunate positions before her mind was put at ease as to the fate of her wine. Splashing mud covered them, leaving their hair in mats and clumps. "Nuts," she muttered, and went about easing the landing of the remaining ones. Green hair seemed to be everywhere. This struck Mother Nature, in her drunken state, as a rather unique and lovely look. She covered the ground with green hair.

Her creative side took hold. Putting hair on the feet of the unfortunate upside-down angels, Mother Nature chuckled. Awesome. She'd call them treeze. Treeeeze. Her inebriated mind liked the sound of that.

Then she remembered there was a serious matter at hand. Furious, she turned back to her counterpart, who she blamed for the mess on her planet.

"This," she blew in a hissing stream, sending God rolling time over teakettle, "this for Your precious lists and forms. They won't help this time. Look what I've had to do with my planet because of You! She straightened to her full height, an impressive feat. "You just watch," she said. "I'm gonna *rock* this world!"

As a matter of fact, I'm declaring this planet my own. I'm moving down here, right now, and from now on You can create Your planets by Yourself. And," she huffed, "You as much as put one foot on *my* planet, and I'll hit you with a restraining order. Got it?"

Without waiting for an answer, she summoned her things about her, and moved to the planet. Peering up, she could still see the crestfallen look on God's face, so she put fluffy curtains all around. Then she settled in. Staring at the never-ending rivers of mead, she hiccupped. "Now concentrate," she said to herself, looking at the liquid. "Fish... fish... fissssssshhhhhhh..."

# SHE

Athens never knew what hit it.

Athens, Nevada was a mirage of a town, a green, lush oasis of happy people, straddling the edge of the desert. It was a small town of a few hundred people, sixteen shops, and an enormous Lodge temple at the end. The temple, Ionic columns and all, had been built by the eccentric old man who started the town, a member of some long-forgotten order of something-or-other. The moment the old man died, the town turned it into a combination post office, community center, and town hall.

In Athens, people waved to each other, children and dogs ran wild, and everyone knew everybody's business. It had been that way since its conception, unaltered. Each day the same, each week, each decade, until the day *she* arrived, and everything changed.

She appeared, seemingly out of nowhere on a summer Tuesday. No one saw her arrive; no one saw *how* she arrived. She seemed to be, in one moment, just there. For all anyone knew, she could have flown in on a magic carpet, or been spirited in by the wind, so suddenly did she appear. Looking at her, no-one would have been faulted for thinking that; there was something magical about her.

Exceptionally tall for a woman, she had a delicate body and an imperious bearing. Her bangles made soft, tinkling sounds as she moved. Her dress was long, white and pristine. She exuded a hypnotizing energy. As she walked into the town, she drew every eye.

Athens had never encountered such a remarkable creature before. She could have been a goddess or some mysterious alien being, such was the effect she had.

Everyone who saw her stopped, mesmerized. No one offered assistance or asked why she'd come. They couldn't take their eyes from her. She didn't mention their rudeness; she'd seen it before.

Looks such as hers had been known to cause accidents, and Athens was no exception. A couple of cars swerved into the middle of the street as drivers stared, entranced, crashing into one another. She paid no attention; she knew she was extraordinary.

A Mona Lisa smile sat on rounded red lips; eyes were deep set in her perfect oval of a face. The eyes were unsettling; they were large on her face, and a grey so deep they seemed molten. There was no doubt arcane mysteries hid in them.

Her neck was long and milky white, even in the desert sun. Her ears were delicate, gold drops hanging from small lobes. Her hair, though, was the crowning glory that pulled every eye. Never had been seen hair such as hers. It was as unique as she, herself, was; long, tangled strand upon strand of tiny, exquisite green and brown writhing snakes.

As Medusa entered the temple dedicated to her, there was only the sound of silence.

# DEFYING GRAVITY

In the photos she was a petite woman with an hourglass figure, her breasts so large I wondered how they managed to defy gravity. She was sturdy in a milkmaid sort of way; all the round parts exactly where round parts should go. Her legs were shapely and strong – a sculptor surely would have loved to fashion them in clay. Her face was sweet but strong, with a good smile.

She married the spoiled son of an oil magnate. He had too much money and too little humanity. Her father-in-law, Robert, adored her. He would have liked her to live with him as his daughter through the end of his life. Medora was that kind of woman.

He asked her stay with him in his mansion when things got ugly, but she never did.

Her husband Kenneth was abusive; she was stoic. He lived a dissipated life. She honored her marriage, had three children over a period of eleven years and dealt with the fallout when he was home. He finally divorced her to marry his current girlfriend, a painful blow. I never heard her say a bad word about him.

Behind her back we did it for her.

The divorce left her destitute, embarrassed and ashamed. She moved in with her parents and put herself through nursing school to support the kids. She was a good nurse.

Wherever she went she fought off advances. She was never tempted till she met Jesus. From that point on it was Him and her, right up to the end of her life.

She never considered remarrying because Jesus said it was a sin. Instead, she showed her devotion to Him by becoming a minister. A small, round, foot-stomping preacher in a Pentecostal church. She could bring down fire and brimstone, though she usually went the other way. When she preached, you listened. When she prayed, you felt better. It was just that way. Jesus never thought to refuse her.

Medora turned the other cheek, again and again. She was the epitome of humility and meekness (we used the word 'doormat'), pushed around and used by almost everyone she knew. She gave money and clothing that she could barely afford, cleaned the church every week, made the largest portions of food for the church dinners and babysat children and old folks while others went to have fun. She was never asked to go.

Good Christian people gossiped and told cruel stories about her because she followed her faith so closely. They had good fun and thousands of laughs at her expense. She never said a bad word against any of them, either.

But behind her back, we did it for her.

She worked until her body gave out; then one of those good Christians evicted her from the apartment that she'd called home for decades. Her children purchased a trailer closer to the church, and she walked the mile there and back almost every day. I teased her about it when she was in her mid-sixties.

"You know," I'd say thoughtfully, looking down. "I've got great legs. You've got great legs, too, Nana; still pretty good-looking gams at your age."

She was embarrassed almost to the point of offense by my impropriety, flustered, shoo-shooing me away and speeding up to have time to compose herself.

By this time, although her legs were still shapely from so much walking, her round places were much rounder, and the bra straps holding those huge breasts had burrowed their way into the flesh of her shoulders at least an inch. She still walked with her back held straight, though, and the deep lines caused by the torment that was her life did not overtake the web of fine lines that was her faith.

She lived for another twenty years, although during the last five, she wasn't there. All the bodily and emotional pain plus a series of small strokes were too much for her. Somehow, she escaped from that wonderful body and some other woman, a woman I didn't know, took her place.

She didn't have much to leave when she died. I didn't care. She'd given me her legacy when she was alive. A faith so absolute it was solid as concrete under her feet. Compassion when others felt disgust. Love so all-encompassing no one was excluded. No one at all. The fire opal from one of her father-in-law's mines that I wore at my wedding. The smile that stayed firm through everything. The connection of our hearts. Memories of the times she'd whisper: "you were born for me." The feel of her lap that still held me as an adult when I needed it, and her bosom that pillowed my head while she rocked peace and comfort into me, singing softly. A hundred more intangible things, each one priceless.

I look at her photos every now and then. I still wonder at how she managed to defy the harsh gravity of this world.

# GUINEVERE'S EVOLUTION

Guinevere the Girl –
a fierce fourteen year old with tomboyish tendencies

"Good word, Caelia," exclaimed King Leodegrance. "What is the girl doing? *Why* is she playing with a sword, pretending to be a knight?"

Queen Caelia smiled. "She says she's done with males. Guinevere has made an oath to skewer the next boy that offends her. She's all tomboy, that one, and she's willful, just as is her father."

"She's foolhardy, is what she is. She's acting like a commoner, not a lady. And definitely *not* like a princess. She'll think herself hard done by if she cuts the nose from that beautiful face, and that's just what's going to happen if she keeps this up. She's a teenager now. It's past time for her father to step in and set her straight."

Caelia barely looked up from her needlework. She was of the opinion that Guinevere should be able to defend herself. However, since it was never good to contradict a king, she just said, "Of course dear, you do that." As Leodegrance stalked off, Queen Caelia rolled her eyes and sighed.

"*Princess* Guinevere!" Leodegrance roared as he neared. "Daughter!"

Guinevere startled and turned quickly, sword blade stopping within an inch of her father's nose. Hastily she lowered it and smiled winningly. "Yes, my father?" Leo breathed deeply, calming his pounding heart. If only she'd been a son; she would have made him proud. But a girl...with a sword...eesh.

"*You* are a menace," he growled. "Just what purpose do you think you have with a sword? Why are you wielding this?" he asked, grabbing it from her.

"Why, as you can see, Father, I'm learning to defend myself against idiots. I must teach myself because no one will train me."

A speculative look came into her eyes. "You know Father… there is no one better to learn from than one's King. I would consider myself the luckiest girl in Carmelide if you would train with me." She smiled her winning smile again.

Leo raised his hand. "Don't you try that smile on me, young lady. It will not work. And I most assuredly will not train with you, nor will any man in this kingdom, if he wants to keep his life and lands. A *lady*, a *princess*, wielding a sword! Of all the things!" Leodegrance was outraged.

After a long moment settling himself, his attention shifted to the sword in his hand. He hefted it and looked it over, impressed by the workmanship.

"Whose sword do you use, daughter? It is of marvelous make. Who loaned you such a sword?" Guinevere's mouth tightened. "It's mine," she muttered defiantly, looking away.

"What do you mean, it's yours? From whom did you get this? Exactly whom do I have to thank for my daughter cutting the air with a lethal weapon?"

"I mean, it's mine. It was made for me. And I want it back." She looked at her father's scowling face and reconsidered. "Please."

King Leodegrance frowned. "Where did you find a smith willing to make a sword for you, much less one of this caliber?" he asked.

"Our smith did it."

"Our smith? I will tear off his arms. I will set coals on his tongue and eyes. I will mutilate him!"

"Oh, no, Father!" Guinevere grabbed his arm. "He had no choice in the matter. I commanded him to do so and made him swear he would speak not of it." Her grip tightened. "Being the *master* swordsmith that he is, he fashioned a sword both light enough for my use and beautiful enough for the daughter of the King. He is a loyal subject, Father, and he should be *rewarded* for taking such care for me."

Leodegrance muttered and tried a different tack. "Guinevere, you must be aware this brings disgrace upon me, my princess daughter fighting. Ladies do not fight. Ladies do not need to know *how* to fight. This is why we have knights and lords. If someone has wronged you, it is *our* duty to make it right. Your duties entail needlework, and womanly studies, and of course, making a good marriage. That is all that is required of you. It is the duty of the man to protect and serve, and to mete out punishment if required. You should not worry your beautiful head, nor should you fight."

"But *Father*," wailed Guinevere. "Thomas, son of Aldritch, requested a favour for the upcoming joust from *Lady Celia*, not me, and I was standing *right there!*" Her fourteen-year-old nose scrunched distastefully at the thought. Dramatically waving arms, she continued, "He should have asked *me*; I *am* royalty, you know! And right in front of all those lords;. I am disgraced! I am a laughingstock, Father. I will not be able to show my face for several *years!*

"But while it is true that I want to *gut* that Thomas, it is truer that I want to swing my very own sword. Perhaps,

Father, you would consider, that if no one were to know, I might practice in private? With a knowledgeable master who would see no harm is done, of course. It gives me such pleasure! I am sure such an exercise would bring no disgrace upon the King. Please, Father?"

Leo shook his head, knowing he would eventually capitulate; envisioning with dread his teenage daughter stabbing her suitors. Perhaps he *should* teach her how to use a sword properly in case one decided to fight back. Looking at his sweet Guinevere, he raised, then lowered his hand.

"There are no words for such a thing," he muttered to himself. "No words at all."

Guinevere the Queen –
an enchanting and refined Lady
who has not gutted her husband King

"This is glorious, Arthur," smiled Guinevere. "Our wedding will be the talk of several kingdoms."

"Consider this day of amusements the first of many, my dear," responded Arthur. "I know how much you love entertainments."

The people of the kingdom had organized spectacular amusements for Guinevere's wedding to Arthur. The courtyard was bright with floral decorations; loud with music. Food and wine were free to all. There were jugglers and maidens with posies, acrobats and contortionists. Storytellers perched on great chairs, holding both children and adults in thrall.

In the field, servants were setting up for an archery competition. Pages were grooming horses before the coming joust. Later there would swordsmanship demonstrations, running at rings, and in the night, fireworks and dancing. Knights would give her their allegiance, poets and bards give forth with magnificent voice. It would be a very long day of pleasure. Guinevere smiled again, squeezing Arthur's arm.

It was hours later, just as the jousting was to begin, that Guinevere finally succumbed. Arthur looked concerned, but she reassured him. "It is but a response to the excitement of the day, my King," she said. "With your permission, I will take my ladies and retire for a short rest."

He touched her hand. "Shall I put a halt to the festivities until you return, then? I want this day to be perfect for you, dear. You will miss some of the finest jousting in three kingdoms. No one can compare to Camelot knights, you know."

Guinevere smiled. "Thank you for your thoughtfulness, husband, but I expect to watch our exalted knights many times in future. Let me take my leave now that I may enjoy later events rested; and since I believe jousting is *your* favorite part of the festivities, I will not hold you any longer. Call forth your champions, my King!" With a small curtsy and a smile, she placed her hand on the arm of one of her ladies and walked slowly down the dais. Arthur watched until she entered a small tent, then turned his attention back to the field.

\* \* \*

"Release me from these hundred pounds of clothing, ladies, please," Guinevere entreated. "Let me be free to breathe!" She stood motionless while they undressed her down to her shift, then took deep breaths. One of her ladies-in-waiting brought her bread and a vessel of spiked wine, while her personal maid brought forth another set of clothing.

She drank deeply, then stretched. "Freedom at last! I might have been wearing lead, for the weight of all these garments. And once more I don a hundredweight," she joked, standing serenely as her maids pulled and pushed and dressed her. "Bye the bye," she asked, "how many knights joust today?"

"Twelve, my Queen," answered Elaine, her personal maid, as she settled the helmet over Guinevere's head and checked her straps.

Raising the eyepiece, Guinevere looked at her. "And which one will I have the honor of knocking off his horse?"

"A handsome fellow," her maid smiled. "They say his name is Lancelot."

*Author Intro*

# JONATHAN LANGDON

I am single, 81, and live with my one-eyed cat, Mikey, of whom I've written several poems.

I was born, raised, educated (BA in history, University of California, Berkely,1965) and spent four years in the U.S. Navy. Most of my life was spent in the San Francisco Bay area, born in San Francisco, raised in Palo Alto,, fourteen years in Berkeley, and about thirty years out on the Point Reyes Peninsula in Marin County, where I was a general building contractor. I have several ex-wives, two  grown-up kids and two grand kids.

Twice I have lived in Port Townsend for a total of ten years. I am an artist and a poet, having been published in the *West Marin Review* as a poet, a prose writer, and an artist, in the *Point Reyes Light,* and in the anthology of poems *There's A Thread You Follow* published by the Quimper UU Fellowship of Port Townsend.

The spirits move me to write and paint, sometimes a lot and sometimes not at all. I never know, but am always ready to answer the call.

Contact Jonathan at Jonathanlangdon114@yahoo.com

## A DIFFERENT SORT

Drink in hand,
on my porch,
lingering in the last warmth of a summer day,
a little bird hops into my yard,
just six feet away.

I twerp and tweet at him,
pretending to say hello.
He turns without a sound,
head cocked,
stares at me for the longest time,
taking me in,
answering in his own way.
Then he hops and I sip,
each returning to his own task.

Something has passed between us,
not hello,
but a recognition of the other,
communication of a different sort
that warms me more
than the lingering heat
of that hot summer day.

# ANY SONG WILL DO

At home, alone,
all by myself,
touched by a tune on the radio,
I start to sing a silly song,
made up on the spot,
my cat looking on,
as if to say "I don't understand,
but I feel like purring."

This brings us together,
in a nonsensical language of a muse
that touches each of us in its resonance,
without labeling,
and without the tyranny of words.

I've seen a video of a man
playing a piano in a field and
how his cows came running over the rise
at the first few notes.

I know of some farmers who play Beethoven or Bach
to sooth their cows in the milking sheds.
I don't know what, if anything,
it does for the butterfat content of the milk,
but it matters not,
the men and their cows seem content.

Likewise, my cat and I revel in each other,
he purring, I singing,
sharing in something
neither of us understands,
but sharing,
nevertheless.

## IT MATTERS NOT

I went to Island Marrowstone
to watch the anglers ply their trade,
cast and catch with accolade.
As I gazed upon the waters blue,
my thoughts again returned to you.
I had visions of you naked on my bed,
bent arm as pillow for your head,
with splayed out breasts and silky hair.
both on top
and, well,
you know where.

We're no longer beauties you and I,
one look, and we can't deny,
the ravages of time and place.
There are wrinkles, there are sags,
there are liver spots, and there are tags.

It matters not,
we're not confused,
as we look upon the naked other
with eye bemused.
We see beyond the flesh outside
to that tender inner spot where love resides,
recognizing all the while,
that these few words,
while clearly heard,
are just mere tokens
of the many words still yet unspoken.

*Author Intro*

# DEREK HUNTINGTON

I was born and raised on the Olympic Peninsula. I spent many summers hiking mountain and beach trails while questioning life's many mysteries. Writing down my thoughts has brought me a clearer understanding of the perplexities in living. Writing is my therapy and as I grew I came to realize that I could express myself through writing when I couldn't convey my thoughts and feelings verbally.

I enjoy history, sports, and reading. Stephen King is my favorite. Family is also an important component in my life. I have a wife and six year-old-daughter.

Thank you for reading. "Playing God" won a ribbon at the fair.

Contact Derek on Facebook and email  at
derekh_1985@hotmail.com.

# PLAYING GOD

We make genetically modified organisms,
And turn them into new plants and foods.
Is that like us playing God?
Should we be doing it?
Is it right?
Is it what he'd want?
Will there be consequences?

We neuter and spay animals,
And ourselves.
Is that like us playing God?
Should we be doing it?
Is it right?
Is it what he'd want?
Will there be consequences?

Women use birth control as a way to prevent babies,
And some have abortions.
Is that like them playing God?
Should they be doing it?
Is it right?
Is it what he'd want?
Will there be consequences?

Many people myself included have all different types of pets,
And there are zoos all over the world,
Where people can go to see animals,
Without having to go to their natural habitats.
Is that like us playing God?
Should we be doing it?
Is it right?
Is it what he'd want?
Will there be consequences?

We cross breed animals and also make new species of animals.
Is that like us playing God?
Should we be doing it?
Is it right?
Is it what he'd want?
Will there be consequences?

We get surgeries to repair part of our bodies when needed.
We get immunizations to keep us from getting certain sicknesses.
And take medicine that we invented when we get sick.
Is that like us playing God?
Should we be doing it?
Is it right?
Is it what he'd want?
Will there be consequences?

Some change their sex type,
And increase and/or reduce their breast size.
Is that like us playing God?
Should we be doing it?
Is it right?
Is it what he'd want?
Will there be consequences?

We sentence people to death,
And eventually end their life.
Is that like us playing God?
Should we be doing it?
Is it right?
Is it what he'd want?
Will there be consequences?

In life sometimes accidents or other events happen,
That force a person to make the decision,
Of whether or not to pull the plug.
Or put our pets to sleep.
Is that like us playing God?
Should we be doing it?
Is it right?
Is it what he'd want?
Will there be consequences?


We chop down trees and use them to build houses,
And make many other things.
We build roads and destroy the natural habitats of many animals.
Is that like us playing God?
Should we be doing it?
Is it right?
Is it what he'd want?
Will there be consequences?


We take so many things,
And change them from what they naturally where,
And I question.
Is it like us playing God?
Should we be doing it?
Is it right?
Is it what he'd want?
Will there be consequences?
In the end will it matter?
Am I the only one who thinks about this?
Does no one care?


Are we playing God...?
Should we be...?

*Author Intro*

# ROBERT THOMPSON

I was born an army brat which means I've been on the move most of my life. I was born in Texas but started school in Germany; by the third grade I was back in the USA to see my first TV in Fort Carson, Colorado.

In time I married in Houston, became a Christian in Kansas City, and helped deliver four babies by home-birth. Along the way, I gave up alcohol and worked as a Peace Officer in California, all before moving to the Olympic Peninsula.

One thing that has never changed is my love of reading. Sit me down with C.S. Forrester, Zane Grey or Mark Twain, and I'm a happy camper.

Contact Robert at elalemano.thompson@gmail.com

# IT BEARS THINKIN'

A short while ago, I discovered that we had a raccoon or two in our yard. Homeless, of course. At least they weren't begging and bothering us (yet).

I went out into my backyard to clean/ inspect a swing I had built for our granddaughter last year. We were expecting company and our friends had a toddler that might like that. Some do, you know. Anyway, while I was looking around to remove stickers and such, I noticed some poop at the foot of the tree next to where the swing was. I called my neighbor over to ask what it was, and he surmised that it was a raccoon or two.

My wife didn't believe him and posted a query on Facebook. She got lots of valuable free advice. She thought it might be a bear. My neighbor said that's half right since a raccoon is part of the bear family (a dubious claim for sure - like claiming a small dog is a cat).

One worthy said to dig up all the "evidence" and put it in a plastic bag, pour Clorox in the hole, and that would take care of it. Another man said that won't help at all, but to circle the tree seven times blowing a trumpet, and the raccoon/bear would fall out of the tree. When we got done laughing at that one, another said to get night vision goggles and shoot it. I asked my neighbor about that idea, and he said, "The law clearly says that you can't shoot at a moving vehicle for fear that you'd injure someone in the crowd!" I wasn't sure what the crowd was, but I was really perplexed about the moving vehicle. I decided that my neighbor was really rowing with one oar, and to ignore his advice.

Another magic phone advise was to put a bear trap at the foot of the tree on all four sides, and that would settle it. I didn't have the heart to do that, so we kept looking. One woman said that if we cut a bunch of thorn branches from the blackberry bushes, and circled the tree with that, they'd leave after a few days. It may sound strange, but we decided to go cut some thorns and do that. It didn't cost much. After we did that, my neighbor told us, "It's lucky you weren't caught, for poaching the king's blackberries is against the law!" Poaching? Really? We heard that ya'll had very intrusive laws in this State, but that seemed too much. It turned out that he was pulling our leg.

We had dinner that night and watched some tv, and tried to forget all about it, but then my wife noticed that the conversation on Facebook continued, and she had some seventeen entries since we stopped looking. We read them... get a dog and put him in the back yard (that'd be fine, but we don't want a dog, and it'd still be there when the raccoons were gone)...shoot it with a BB gun! You can't even see them in the tree, and I'm supposed to shoot them?

We cleaned the mess twice and washed up good after, cause someone said that there were some fierce roundworms that're worse than death to get, and raccoons carry them around everywhere they go. We doused the spot with Clorox too, even though these super worms were immune to Clorox, they said.

If they don't go away soon, we may get a trumpet and march around the tree seven times just in case.

*Author Intro*

# CAROLYN PARKER

As an amateur behind the pen, I am grateful for the friendly and supportive writing community in Sequim where I live January to May escaping winters in Maine. While the Sequim snow of 2019 surprised us all, that magnificent storm inspired resilience in many forms.

A nature lover at heart, I enjoy walking, hiking, swimming and dancing—so much pleasure within minutes of my SunLand home! Summers and autumns I write from my kayak on the Presumpscot River in Windham, Maine.

Contact Carolyn at carolynparkerlmt@gmail.com

# AWAKENING

## by Hood Canal

Yahweh of the morning light
entwined with breath and touch just right
the  Force bringing waves to body and shore
loving

Below on beach, man and dog
raindrops part of their lolling stride
our eyes meet the beckoning tide
strangers

Strangers only for lack of a name
within our cells it is all the same
the brine of the ocean, the salt of our blood
one mind

Wind under wings of gulls
the same wind that freshens our step
the air that becomes our breath
living

# A DUNGENESS MEMORY

High above the Strait of Juan de Fuca's shore
I walk along a path that calls me evermore.
Blasted by gale force wind driven rains
high sandy banks
  wear down
    cave in
      topple trees twisted by wind.
WARNING signs are posted where once there were none.
Pathways divert away from the view.

A striking photo of this beach and a man
taken from a place I can no longer stand
graces my wall proving once I was there
where the bank disappeared from this spot in mid air.
Gone! I *miss* it, yet wonder survives —
the wonder of nature, its beauty and fury
making treasures of memories I consider with awe.

The path as it is now remains for our pleasure.
Follow my footsteps — go for a hike
before where we stand disappears in the sand.

# RESILIENCE

I thought the burning bush was a goner
the way it leaned densely laden
shouldering its burden
of heavy, wet snow.

So, too, the laurel hedge overgrown
bent low with snow
two branches broken.

After days encumbered
I lifted arm loads of snow.
Branches sprang up with great force.
I heard sighs of relief.

This morning
the burning bush dazzles
with diamond droplets
gems of every hue
blues, greens, ruby reds
and now — a flash of gold!*

Promises of spring branch forth
finger-like tips pinking
reaching out new with life.

*Sunlight refracts colorfully through water droplets on branches, leaves, and needles of trees after a rain or snow melt and in grass and spider webs on a dewy morning — a beautiful and natural phenomenon.

## SPRING ON THE WING

Spring is on the wing—or so they say
no matter lingering snow that came our way.
This back drop of white is in perfect array
for red breast of robin and blue of stellar jay.

The gutter on the house across the street
is lined with robins—my breakfast treat
for they ate all my holly berries then beat feet.

# TEN MINUTES AFTER

Ten minutes after I get up
I return to make my bed.
Sheets and pillow warm
even as I will be
ten minutes gone.

How will my life be different *today*
than ten minutes after and still warm?

*Author Intro*

# JAN THATCHER ADAMS, MD

I was privileged to practice womb to tomb family medicine for 25 years, gathering the gifts of stories along the way. After that, I turned to Emergency Medicine, and now, in 2019, am preparing to retire from Olympic Medical Center, with a total of 47 years of medical practice and healing about to be behind me. I shall miss it terribly, but it is time to step down. I will be forever grateful for the joy this profession has brought me, and the deep richness of sharing in the lives of those who came to me.

All the while, along the way, I continued my family's tradition of writing, authoring scores of published articles as well as my autobiographical book *Football Wife Coming of Age with the NFL*. It chronicles my marriage to a football player during the wild formative years of the NFL.

After 42 years of enjoying Minnesota, except for the ticks and mosquitoes, I relocated to this corner of paradise, which I share with my husband and three cats. I'm enjoying the abundant writing community, playing my cello in the amazing symphony, and displaying my art at the One of a Kind gallery.

The autobiography *Football Wife Coming of Age with the NFL* was published in 2011 and is available on Amazon.

Jan can be reached at jantadams@aol.com

# POLLY

A charming, mischievous toddler,
She brings me shredded toilet paper
From the adjacent room
And cavorts about as
Her mom and I talk.

Polly had a brief low fever
Two hours earlier
But it is gone now.
She also got a nasal flu dose today,
As her sister has influenza.
Although late, her mom
decided to immunize her for the season.

She has no cough
Or vomit
Or diarrhea.

I examine her.
She is completely normal,
A lively, delightful little person.

Two days later I return to this hospital site.
All the staff is watching me.
Something is wrong.

One day after I saw Polly,
An ambulance screamed in
With her in extremis,
Her seizing little body

Unalert, frothing at the mouth.

The doctor could not save her.
The entire hospital grieved
and attended her funeral.

Influenza—double dose
From her sister and also the too late immunization
Killed her, according to the pathologist.

Nothing in life is guaranteed,
Not even that bright little charmers
Will live to beguile another day.

# SAM

His tummy waged war,
With steady cramps, vomit, and diarrhea.
He fell from toilet to floor,
In a sweaty faint.

Shortly, he awoke to his dog
Licking his behind.

Later, In the Emergency room,
I said,
"Now that's a real service dog!"

With much laughter,
We all set about his healing.

# JACK

Schizophrenia is a chameleon
Chewing on its victims in relentless torture
Especially when medications are tossed out.

Jack, brought to the ER by police,
Is violently paranoid and hallucinating.
He is shouting disconnected words and thoughts,
And hitting, kicking, biting
All who try to bring him some relief.

He must be restrained for a time,
And provided a critical injection
To calm his inflamed mind and body.

It works-he is so tired.
He sleeps, out of restraints.
He wakes, and devours a meal.

Though closely observed,
He suddenly strips and
Sprints, buck naked,
into another department,
Seriously alarming a raft
of patients and nurses.

Security attempts to corral him,
But, with a stunned audience,
he just flops on his back and spread-eagles
on the cool floor.

Eventually four strong men,
Each lifting a rigid limb,
Manage to muscle this wild, naked man
Back to the ER, for  restraints and another shot,
Leaving a trail of folks behind who will
Sure have something to discuss
Over dinner.

As for Jack, he will spend
The next many weeks,
Locked somewhere in a psych ward,
Getting back on his medicines.

They say schizophrenia "burns out"
When its victims age past sixty or seventy.
Until then, this stricken young man
Will rage, rage against the
Merciless Voices
in his brain.

## JOSEPH'S HEART

It was his third heart attack,
At 89, he knew his time grew short.
There remained no further surgeries,
Medicines, or stents
That could help.

Today is Friday,
and his wildly beating heart
Is keeping me and the staff busy
With treatment.

But, he has a full family reunion tomorrow,
And he is pleading to go.
I repeatedly tell him
His heart will not allow it.

Finally, he says
"I'd rather die of a heart attack
Than a broken heart!"

I heard that message.
I explain to him how to
Sign out Against Medical Advice
In the morning,
And we agree on ways
for him to rest and minimize
The chance of disaster.

Three weeks later I return to
This hospital for more shifts.

I am thrilled to see him in the clinic,
Terrible shape as usual,
Regaling me with stories from
This, his last earthly reunion.

The heart speaks
A strong language,
And must be heard.

# GRETA

In the tight aisle airline seat,
I am across from an elderly lady.

The flight attendant brings boiling hot coffee,
And it spills in Greta's lap.

I am up immediately to help.
We all proceed quickly to the rear of the plane.

Poor Greta is whimpering.
We remove her steaming garments,
To find her lower abdomen, private parts,
and upper legs already blistered.

Ice is applied, and cool moist rags
With some relief.
Pain medicine is available in the flight bag,
And that helps some.

She is awkwardly lying on the crowded floor,
Exposed.
A kind flight attendant
Provides her own dry clothes for cover,
After we loosely swaddle the entire area
With salve and bandages.

She is taken to first class where she can stretch out.
An ambulance meets the plane when we arrive.

Travel disaster-
A risk one takes.

# WAYNE

Urgent pleas for a doctor
Wake me from my uncomfortable
Airline cramped sleep.

At the rear service deck,
I find a ridiculously drunken man
Worried about his headache
And soaring blood pressure.

He has forgotten to take his medicine
And now he is in trouble.
I have him lie down,
A pillow under his red-faced head.
The flight attendant retrieves his carry-on.

I find his medication, and administer a double dose.
A cool cloth to his forehead calms him.
Soon, he sleeps
There on the crowded floor.

I am grateful to monitor his
Blood pressure out of the danger range.
And grateful he
Does not start vomiting!

# GRACE

Her mother, knowing she could not beat
The terrible heroin and crack cocaine habit,
Decided on abortion.
She went to an agency, where the nice lady
Told her the pregnancy was from the grace of god,
And the child would be god's child.

The agency did not have the ability to help with health,
But they provided some diaper coupons
And several nice pamphlets complimenting
Her mother on deciding for life.
So, with no prenatal care, her mom birthed Grace
On the floor of a filthy crack house, barely aware she was
Bleeding to death.

Grace lived in an incubator for two months,
As she painfully withdrew from her drug addiction,
And gained the weight she had not in utero,
due to malnutrition.

Adopted at age 2 by my patient,
Who had a lovely little girl already
And wanted to help this sweet unfortunate child,
Grace seemed charming and delightful.

At age 4 Grace set her sister on fire.
Sister survived, with horrible burns.
When 6 , Grace burned the shed
And stabbed the family dog.

The counselors diagnosed her as psychopath.
She was remanded to institutionalization
Until age 18.
Her parents unadopted her,
Breaking under the financial burden of her care.

At 20 she coldly killed a fellow heroin addict,
Who had a syringe she wanted.
Through all of this,
Where was the nice lady
From the agency
Who made sure this gift from god
Graced the earth?

# NINA

She was a feisty 94,
Lived right across the street from
My clinic.

She and her husband
Emigrated from Russia, and
She was a piano teacher
Until her mid eighties.

She saw me once a year,
Grudgingly.
She called herself
"Just an old vitch!"

As a family doc, I was privileged to care for her,
her elderly husband,
Her daughter and grandchildren.

One day she came for her yearly visit.
She was not on medications and had no complaints.
Her examination was unremarkable
For her advanced age.

She surprised me by asking
If she had heard correctly
From friends that I play the piano and organ.

I affirmed that,
Then she stunned me by
Removing a large pile of Russian piano music from her bag.

When she presented it to me, she said-
"This is for you. I won't need it anymore,
But you will, you'll see."

That night, she died in her sleep.

She never learned that I
Became so involved with Russia
And its culture, I married a Russian man.

He very much enjoys the
Music she gifted me.

# BRUCE

The overhead asks for a doctor, stat.
I rush to the rear of the plane,
And find a flight attendant
On the floor, sweating, pale,
barely conscious.

I ask him questions
About his health
And learn he is an
Insulin dependent diabetic.

He has skipped a meal— too busy.
With his own glucometer
I learn his blood sugar is dangerously low.

The plane medical kit has
The correct injection he needs,
And he is provided orange juice.

We wait and watch as his skin dries,
his color returns, his blood sugar improves.
But he and I both know
he might tank again,
So every 15 minute glucometer readings
must be done for a time.

Sure enough, though he has eaten by now,
He drops too low again.
Another injection fixes him for the duration of the flight.

In an hour, I see him busily providing
Passenger service.

# MARY LOU

We are flying to Russia,
Cramped in our airline seats.

The announcement asks urgently for a doctor.
I quickly respond.

In the flight attendant's bed compartments
I never knew existed,
I find a stricken, ashen, sweating woman,
complaining of crushing chest pain.
A quick exam confirms something dangerous-
Either a heart attack or blood clot to the lungs.
I do what I can with the medicines available,
But say she must get to hospital stat.

We are already over the Atlantic.
The plane must dump its fuel
As it is too heavy to land.

This done, the flight returns to Minneapolis.
Ambulance quick,
She is rushed to hospital.

We are moved to first class!
I learn later she survives.
I am so very blessed
With doctor skills.

## THROUGH THE LACE CURTAINS

### RUSSIA, 2014

An elderly woman walks her dog. She talks to him and pets him as they go, and they take frequent rests. Not because she is tired, but her precious friend, her yellow mutt dog, is severely limping on his right hind leg. By the way he moves, it's clear his right rear hip is agony for him. It is either cancer— most likely—or severe arthritis. Or it could even be an injury from a balcony fall or a fall down the endless flights of stairs in the apartments that hover over this patch of sidewalk. He's not getting veterinary care because she can't afford it, or they might have said to just put him down. She can't even afford any real medical care for herself. And so, like so many living beings in this Potempkin Village called Russia, he, and she as well, will just have to suffer, and then finally die.

A hip young couple, all dressed in black, appear from around the corner and stand in front of a parked car. They each have a cigarette to light. He turns one way to avoid the wind while lighting up, and she turns the other, so that they are a few feet apart, not facing each other. When they both succeed, the smoke drifts from their satisfied lips, but still they don't face each other—they seem lost in reverie. As if on cue, they suddenly turn to each other, all the while completing the ritual of smoking. She talks, he looks at his feet and shuffles them and turns the dusty pavement a bit. She turns back and contemplates the bushes in the small apartment yard. He examines the top of the 12 story building. Again on an unspoken cue, they each take in the last inhale, walk briskly to just beneath my window, throw their cigarette butts there, and walk away.

Ten years later she sees her face in the mirror, the premature wrinkles already forming from the smoking. Twenty years later they have long since grown accustomed to the nasty, juicy chronic smoker's cough. Not long after that, he notes some blood in his sputum—the first message from beyond of his imminent passing from lung cancer. She just keeps on coughing and wonders when she can get a full breath again. For her, the smoke will just rob her of some of her breath with each passing year until she finally chokes and dies for lack of oxygen. And they were such a beautiful young couple.

*Author Intro*

# EVA MCGINNIS

I won a shiny Brownie camera in a Polish language newspaper contest in Detroit in 1960. It was my first published essay. I grew up in a tight-knit community of refugees, who had survived the holocaust. Our lives were centered around the schools and churches and the dynamic Polish/American culture we shared. And so began my fascination with both writing and photography. Both are still like magic blank slates on which I can create worlds that touch hearts and imaginations.

I hold degrees from Michigan State and Iowa State, and a certificate in Poetry from University of Washington. But the true practice of poetry came from the heartfelt interactions in an informal women's writing group which met for eighteen years in the Seattle area. All the while, my career spanned various academic, non-profit and business positions, with plenty of volunteering and raising a family. Now I have the blessing of living on the Olympic Peninsula, with the infinite gifts of nature in my back yard to write about and photograph. My husband and I also create original glass jewelry that reflects this beauty and fill everything with love.

Two books of my poetry have been published: *Wings to my Breath* and *At the Edge of the Earth* (available on Amazon.com) and several works appear in literary books and magazines, including *In the Words of Olympic Peninsula Authors Vol2, Tidepools 2017, 2016 Rainshadow Poetry, Wild Willow Women's Anthology Project, Seattle Poems by Seattle Poets Anthology, Woman as Hero Anthology, A Mother's Touch, Spindrift '93, '94 &'95.*

Eva can be reached at Evapoet@mcginnishome.org

## JACARANDA TREE

In suburban backyard
at the edge of windy canyon,
small birds disappear into canopy
become part of quivering leaves,
some squabble and shove for their turn
at feeders swinging from low branches,
squirrels scamper on lawn, gather overflow.

Hawk swoops
like a windy squall,
birds catch the updraft
lift off in unison.
For a split second
the jacaranda seems
to hover a few inches
above the lawn.
Then the birds scatter,
seek refuge under bushes
down dry canyon slopes.
Tree seems to sink back
as if pulled back by its roots.
Squirrels disappear.

In a gust of silence,
hawk lands on gray fence,
near the now motionless tree
A small bird trapped
in bloodied talons.

Part 2

The hawk steals into my dream
landing on the pale steel railing
of my mother's hospital bed,
where I stood earlier in the day.

Hawk turns his head from side to side
observes her shrunken gray form
sleeping restlessly,
propped by hefty white pillows.
Bruised skin of her hand
pulled taut into a pucker around the
long needle threaded
to bag of dripping fluid.
Clear tube divides her swollen face
dips into her nostrils.
Another discreetly carries away her waste.
Its smell mingles with disinfectant undertow.

No one else sees the silvered hawk,
though the nurses' station is just outside the door
and strained laughter spills over the threshold.

Frantically, I search for cover for Mama.
It's too late to move her.
He won't attack what he cannot see.
As he shifts from one claw to the other
I whip off my sweater and shield her face.
He is startled by my movement,
extends his wings.

As he rises, I lunge in front of him
pull aside the curtain to the next bed,
wave him toward the 92-year-old woman
her mouth wide open, unconscious.

"Let her be the one.
Anyone but my mother!"

I spread out my arms to protect her.
but she is sputtering under my sweater
that has grown into a heavy maroon blanket
embroidered with birds sitting in a jacaranda.
I pull it off in horror.
She is coughing and choking.
When I look back, the hawk is gone.
I awake trembling, my throat dry with sobs

Part 3

The next morning, I'm hesitant to visit
Mama in the hospital.
My sister's presence comforts me.
When we enter, Mama is awake.
I'm astonished at her face,
once heart-shaped,
now distorted into a full moon
by years of medications.

Her cheeks, no longer gray
hold a withered ruddiness.
Though her lips are parched,
her threadbare voice is stronger.
Only the translucent blue eyes remain
as I remember them.

We ask about her night's sleep.
"The woman next to me
screamed during the night.
They took her early this morning
after her heart stopped."

I scan the room
the beating of wings
suddenly in my throat.
I find it hard to breathe
step outside for a few minutes.
There is no sign of the hawk.

When I can speak again with her,
Mama asks us
to bring her a favorite rose,
from the bush
growing by the jacaranda tree.

# ON WRITING POETRY

Poems lure me
with mysterious promises
into hidden whirlpools,
swirling me inside themselves.

An endless trickle
of syllables on my brain
babbling on the borderlands
of awakening
taunting me with moon madness.

They drop me into
blue-ice mountain crevasses
where illusions reflect and splinter
shards of frosted ice-glass
shattered on stone and silence.

Eventually, the streams of words
slow and smooth
into steady cadence,
I hear their music
capable of sculpting river rocks
into a landscape of awakening.

# LABYRINTH

A Wedding Poem
(Epithalamium)

Sacred maze of destiny,
we meet at its edges.
Drawn into the vortex
across distances as vast as that ultimate labyrinth,
the spiral Milky Way.

We peer tentatively over star-strewn hedges
circle cautiously, like orbits of planets
retrace constellations of familiar patterns.

Look inward at self, look outward at self,
eyes seeking confirmation, of trust.
Inching and leaping towards love
already destined in both hearts,
letting the years provide the evidence
that the labyrinth is a safe home,
as intimate as the heart
of the Chambered Nautilus
found at its center.

Every moment, perfect,
in its intricate richness
where falling down means startling awake,
illness, a sharpening of gratitude for privilege
of being allowed to walk this journey.

Today, our steps are bold,
hands entwined, rings blessed.
Hesitation banned outside
the rose mandala
of family's protective embrace.
Eyes no longer averted,
but glowing with conviction
that this labyrinth is,
at last, the only path,
to the Beloved.

## MAMA'S CHICKEN SOUP

Even though it's July,
I simmer the chicken on the stove
till the chunks of meat
fall away from bones.
I dice carrots into tiny cubes,
dunk a whole onion into the broth
let its juices leach out, then throw it away.
Just like she did.

She would have insisted
on plenty of her homemade
egg noodles or dumplings
to swivel around in the soup,
topped with chopped parsley.

As children we were permitted
to eat only after blessing the food
and she made the sign of the cross,
on the bottom of a thick loaf of rye bread
with her big knife, from one end of the loaf
to the other and back across.
She said it was what her mother had done.
Then she spread pale butter on the bread.

She was proud of her chicken soup,
rich with floating golden rings of fat,
prepared at least once a week
throughout my childhood,
a symbol of abundance in America.

Now I bless the soup pot on my stove,
quietly steeping its fragrance
into the pores of my home,
on this anniversary of her death.

# MORNING AFTER
# FEBRUARY SNOWFALL 2019
## (Olympic Peninsula)

Twenty-eight hours of steady snowfall.
Evergreens strain under their thick loads
frozen branches arc low
into the satin morning sheen.
Pearl-white stillness muffles the creek below.

After snow clouds disperse,
the wind saunters through valley
lifts powder from topmost branches.
Liberated snowflakes take flight,
to neighboring trees or circle back to lower boughs.

As the sun joins in, stronger gusts shudder trees
which release steamy billows,
micro-jewel droplets shimmer
into shapeshifting clouds,
white dolphin leaping into a donut hole
a swooping bird of prey under slice of sunlight.

Occasionally, swaying branches
release large clumps of snow, which avalanche
onto lower limbs till they plop on the padded ground.
Mists, like gossamer showers waft
into microsecond waterfalls
magnificent in their hazy freefall
backlit by the low winter sun.

Carrot-shaped icicles drip their sparkling lights
to their own staccato rhythms,
while others crack and spike off quickly
reckless in their own demise.

By mid-afternoon the firs undulate with relief,
swing more freely in the updraft of ascending sprays.
Icy clouds parade again on the horizon.
All in motion to prepare for the second storm,
on its way tonight.

## DANGER, STRONG CURRENT!

Narrow river shimmers charmingly,
its exposed rocks slippery beneath their moss caps.
But we step on solid boulders near the shore
where our boots hold us solid to the earth.
I take them off and soak my blistered feet,
you seem immersed in rushing peace.
Later, we scoff at the hysterical warning sign.

But add some mist or rain,
a slight misstep on the wet rocks,
legs entangled in the grayness,
current will grab you into the rocky chasm
just beyond the stone bridge
like a downed tree limb
over a thousand feet of spectacular falls.

## DANGER, STRONG WHIRLPOOLS!

I meet you on the edge of my departure.
Strong remembrance of lifetimes together
draws us together like the vortex
suction of a fervent current.
You stand proud and solid
in your innocent trust of our destiny.

I teeter and crash in the undertow,
bump into old snags and deadheads,
eddy around jagged whirlpools, for years
tossing in the wounded belly of my fears.
Finally, I'm too exhausted,
cry out in surrender, abandon
to the void, like before my first breath.
I know I am dying
as I ricochet over the falls,
a mere leaf tossed and drowning.

When I land on the slippery rocks,
I find I am bruised, but joyously alive
as if for the first time.
You are there, waiting and smiling.
I look into your limitless eyes.
I now understand - our immortality.

*Author Intro*

## LOUISE LENAHAN WALLACE

I always knew I wanted to write, but never believed I could do it "for real." My first novel took twenty-five years to be published. Thankfully, the next four came more rapidly. In addition to receiving several writing awards, my non-fiction articles have been included in *Chicken Soup for the Single's Soul*, in Chicken Soup's *The Joy of Christmas*, in Peninsula College's *Tidepools*, and in *Grit* Magazine. My advice to beginning writers, "Don't give up your dream of writing." I received enough rejection slips to paper *two* walls before my first novel was published. But when it happened, it was exactly the right time and place.

My novels include *Length of Days, Day Unto Day, Children of the Day, Longing of the Day* and *Day Star Rising*.

The events in "To Hear the Light" took place in Sequim, where my husband and I, with our two daughters, moved in 1977.

Contact Louise at lwallace@olympus.net

# TO HEAR THE LIGHT

Memories. So ephemeral, so fragile, yet so strong that a touch, a fragrance can carry one on the breath of time backward to vanished days and nights. On just such an evening, I stand gazing upward at the blue-black shawl tucked around the shoulders of the world — a mantle stitched together with thread fashioned from a million speckles of starshine.

With a wisp of breeze brushing my cheek, I return to a summer night nearly four decades gone. There, I stand on the front porch with my husband, awe-filled at the immensity of which I am so small a part. Hearing a two-toned rasping, I ask him what it is. Shrugging matter-of-factly, he says it's the young frogs croaking in the field near the lumber yard across Third Street, the same as they always do. Flicking me a puzzled glance, he goes inside. Alone in the velvet darkness, I take in the whisper of the breeze rustling the leaves of the cherry tree on the far side of the lawn, the rush of water in the kitchen sink, the clink of plates as my daughters wash the dishes. At my feet, the cat, swatting at a moth, misses and crashes into the peony bed beside the porch. Thrashing and swearing mark his outward progress. Wearing my first pair of hearing aids, for a long time I stand on the porch and listen to the night.

At the age of two, a high fever accompanying the measles affected my hearing. No one realized it for several years because it wasn't a complete hearing loss. I was simply the "shy, quiet one with her nose always in a book." Many memories of my childhood "non-hearing" experiences have dimmed. Occasionally, however, I am in a group of conversing adults who begin laughing, and I have no clue what is so amusing. In such moments I am transported back to a group of happily chattering girls who all, except for me, suddenly burst into giggles. As with so many other life changes, I accepted my diminished hearing, not realizing it should be any different.

In adulthood, a fluke in the form of my family history, stepped in. On my maternal side, Mom, my aunts and uncle had experienced a decrease in hearing, acute enough to require hearing aids. In my early thirties, I became aware that people around me were talking even more softly than usual and that if someone speaking to me turned around and walked away, still talking, only the voice, not the words, drifted back to me. It became one of those "I suppose I should have my hearing tested" times that I kept putting off because I was busy and knew I couldn't afford hearing aids even if it turned out I needed them.

One afternoon I was leafing through the newspaper and saw a notice for a free hearing test. *I can do that*, I told the empty living room. After all, free wouldn't cost me anything just to find out. I called for an appointment, not realizing I had made a decision whose seconds out of time would remain in my mind as clearly as any event recaptured when someone asks, "Where were you when...happened?" They name a political or national event, and the response of the mind and heart is instantaneous.

At the appointed time, with butterflies performing aerial dives in my stomach, I walked downtown to the VFW Hall on Washington Street for the hearing examination. With a smile and a firm handshake, Roger came forward to meet me and ushered me into the testing room. Realizing that all the "what ifs" I had industriously been manufacturing would soon have answers, I sat on the edge of the chair as one more question prodded me. *Do I really want to know what this checkup is going to show?* My life fit into my world as I now knew it. *What will I do if the results change that?*

Roger carefully arranged headphones over my ears. He motioned toward a clear window in front of me that looked into another room, and I could see a lumpy machine poking up near the glass. He explained he would go in there, press buttons and turn knobs and I was to raise my right or left hand when I heard a tone. He then smiled reassuringly and disappeared around the corner, emerging a moment later behind the glass. I watched as he began pressing keys. I waited, straining to hear something, anything, to which I could respond, but no sound reached either of my ears. He glanced up at me and pushed a few more buttons. Still nothing. He looked at me questioningly and I shook my head. With an expression somewhere between bemusement and determination, he bent over the machine. At last I heard a faint drone in my left ear. With overwhelming relief, I shot my hand up. He nodded, a smile tugging at the edges of his calm demeanor. We finished the test with much button-pressing on his part and intermittent hand-raising on mine. When he came back to my side of the room, he said simply, "You really should be wearing hearing aids." Not pressuring me, just stating a fact.

Now I must decide whether to go on as I had been or alter my life from that day forward. *Missed whispers...and laughter I could not share in...*I took a deep breath. Hearing aids would be expensive, but not nearly as costly as missing out on all the sounds of life going on around me.

Roger took measurements, and several days later I went back to try on my new "ears." He carefully arranged them and stepped back expectantly. For the first time in my memory, noise rushed at me from all sides. The whirring of the office fan. Traffic swishing by on the street outside. Roger's dog, curled up in the corner, snoring lustily. It was rather daunting after so many years of quiet. But it was also a moment of sheer amazement. *This* was what other people heard, *all the time*? By the expression on Roger's face, I wasn't sure which of us was more delighted as I took in the sounds and he took in my joy at hearing them. He assured me that, after a few days, as I got used to them, the heightened level would drop.

The intensity was unnerving at first. Doors shutting cracked as if they had been slammed by a giant's fist; water running in the kitchen faucet fell into the stainless steel sink as loudly as any waterfall I'd stood near; and the turning of newspaper pages crackled like Fourth of July firecrackers exploding.

That evening I stood on the front porch and absorbed the sounds of a hearing world, glad that I had reached out, deeply thankful for the new-found reverberations around me.

I worked nights at the Sequim Nursing Center, and arriving for my shift just before eleven o'clock, I found that my co-workers were delighted that I was finally discovering so much that I had been missing even in normal conversation. But the cost persisted in jabbing at me with pesky fingers.

Taking my usual route home in the morning, I drove toward the sunrise. I was tired and not really thinking about the logistics of getting to the house. I idly pondered who had had the idea for the first hearing device, and when. Did that person ever really grasp what a beacon of light that invention would become to people like me? I would no longer have to stand back, wondering what had sparked a burst of amusement, but could join in the sounds surging around me.

I suddenly realized that a sharp tapping was coming from near the region of the hood. With a husband who repaired cars for a living, he constantly stressed that if I heard *any* strange noises while I was driving, I was to tell him immediately. Obediently I leaned toward the steering wheel. The tapping grew louder. Thankfully, none the gages on the dash showed red, but one on the left side of the panel was definitely glowing green. As I watched it blink on and off, my head finally joined my heart in knowing that I had made the right choice in choosing to wear hearing aids.

Preparing to make a left turn, without thinking, I had pushed the signal lever down. The green indicator light flashed on and off, keeping perfect time with the mysterious ticking. I had always known that the green light blinked when signaling a turn. But until that moment, I had had no idea that it also ticked.

I drove on home, the strengthening dawn light no match for the bright joy welling in my heart.

*Author Intro*

# MIKE NOLAN

A native Washingtonian, I spent the first fifteen years of my life as an Army brat, moving from military base to military base. When my folks retired to Sequim, I attended high school here, graduating in 1973.

I have worked as a short order cook at Nolan's Drive-In, as a commercial clam digger on Sequim Bay, and as a sandblaster in the Seattle shipyards before settling into a thirty-year career as a school guidance counselor. I am retired and live with my wife, Ann, in Port Angeles, where we enjoy hosting our children and grandchildren.

Mike can be reached at mikenolan@olympus.net

# ON-THE-JOB TRAINING

On the day my life was going to end, Davis growled at me. "We got a job to do here." He fixed me with a hard, penetrating stare and jerked his thumb over his shoulder. "Are you the one gonna blast that son of a bitch?"

I blinked and adjusted my hard hat. Standing on the wooden pier, the foreman and I turned to face 3000 tons of haze-gray steel floating in the water. The USS *Roark*, a sleek, 400 foot long Navy frigate, was outlined against a cloudless blue sky. "Sure, I can handle it." I wondered if that sounded as confident as I tried to look.

The heavyset foreman never stopped pushing, shifting his bulk, shoving people around with his words. "I'm serious—serious as a heart attack," was one of his favorite lines. I didn't like Davis, but cared about his opinion of my work. After sandblasting in the shipyards along the Seattle waterfront for a few months, I half-way believed I possessed the skills to do this job. This was my chance to show the foreman I had the chops as a sandblaster, and maybe convince myself at the same time.

I heard the breeze winnow through the metal rigging, and my gaze wandered up along the superstructure and tower to the crow's nest, a hundred feet in the sky. That's where I'd start. "That crow's nest is nothin' more than a grated metal platform with a railing runnin' round it," Davis said, "easy to blast once you're up there."

"No problem."

"Then you just work your way down," he added.

The morning felt warm for spring, with enough sunshine to heat the creosote pilings where we stood. The marine alchemy of softened tar and salty sea air created one of the few pleasant smells in the shipyard, and it drifted over the surface of Elliott Bay, the momentary serenity of the scene at odds with what lay ahead.

Staring at the tower, Davis let out a long breath. "Okay then, do it. Get suited up." In a rare moment of helpfulness he added, "Richards is running the sand pot over on the fantail. I'll tell him you're getting ready." Extending himself meant only one thing: Davis was damn relieved to hand this job off to someone.

There were a half dozen sandblasters at Lockheed Shipyard on Harbor Island, and I was the youngest and least senior, with the next guy possessing at least ten years' experience on me. I knew Davis wanted me to do this particular job after overhearing his conversation with an older blaster, who said, "Now, why would I wanna drag my ass up that tower? Ask the kid to do it. . . hell, he *wants* the work."

That much was true. *The Kid*—me—was the guy who craved more experience. I wanted to run with the old pros, to make sandblasting look easy like they did, but I knew that wouldn't happen overnight. The best I could hope for was to blast everything I could lay my hands on, bust my ass doing it, and down the road hear something like, "You gotta give the kid credit..."

Thirty minutes later I scaled the superstructure and tower in full sandblasting gear. The morning had continued to warm and it was ten degrees hotter inside the heavy, black rubber sandblaster's hood. Sweat ran down my head to the back of my neck, and the two-by-four-inch plate-glass window I looked through fogged up, providing gauzy tunnel vision. *I haven't even started blasting and I'm already winded.* After crawling through the trapdoor to the crow's nest and pulling myself onto the metal deck, panting, I sat listening to my airline clear the plate glass, swiveling my head around to take in the view.

*Jesus, I'm up high.* Looking out beyond the shipyard, past Elliott Bay, the downtown skyscrapers gleamed silver and black in the midmorning sun. Farther out, the sprawl of the city carpeted the hillsides. *Is that Bellevue?* The Cascade Mountain Range hemmed the landscape in, and its mammoth jewel, Mount Rainier, dominated in the south.

*Time to get to work.* I waved to the sand pot tender, Richards, signaling to fire me up. Raising the steel nozzle over my head and bending the hose in an arc against my shoulder, I pressed the trigger, and the deafening rush of sand created a billowing black cloud of grit enveloping the crow's nest. Now I was in my own world.

Everything above the superstructure of the ship is aluminum and, being softer than steel, required only a quick, light blast. *Knock this sucker out...show that oversized bastard you've got what it takes.* Working as fast as possible along the railing, I turned to blast the first post. With both hands on the hose, I stepped to cross the deck of the crow's nest, but my foot didn't touch anything. I was in the air.

"OH GOD! OH GOD! OH GOD!"

I stepped through the open trapdoor of the crow's nest, and was in free fall, a hundred feet up, about to splatter on the ship's deck.

The fall happened in an instant but somehow everything seemed to slow down. My perceptions became elastic, and the moment stretched out long enough for me to watch the crow's nest railing pass by. A steady stream of sand sprayed out in front of me from the hose I still clutched.

An incredible jolt hit my side and lower back. "*AAAAGH.*" My neck whiplashed, and my arms and legs ricocheted upward in opposition to the force. The hose flew out of my hands, flaying wildly. Then my body stabilized, and I hung in the air sideways, six feet below the crow's nest.

Realizing I had automatically clipped my safety harness to the railing upon reaching the crow's nest, I dangled from the nylon strap like a puppet on a string. *Jesus Christ!* The unconscious *click* of the harness carabiner kept me alive. I slowly turned in the gentle morning breeze, defining a lazy arc. God, my side hurt. The tower and ladder came back into view through the plate glass, as I reached out for the reassuring touch of the railing. *Head up, feet down.* My side and back were on fire.

Grabbing a rung, I lined up my body with the tower and stepped onto the ladder. Far below my boots, the upturned faces of a dozen workers gazed back at me, uncharacteristically frozen in the normally chaotic work shift. On the fantail, Richards stared at me too, open mouthed. He cut the pressure at the sand pot and the blasting hose hung flaccid, swaying by my side.

I climbed hand over hand back into the crow's nest, and pulled up the sandblasting hose. *Here I am, trying to impress the foreman,* I thought, *and if I don't wise up and take it easy, I'm going to kill myself.* This time I closed the metal trapdoor behind me. Ignoring the workers below, I made a lasso motion to Richards, indicating I was ready to start again. He charged the hose, and I began to blast where I left off.

It only took a couple minutes to overcome the surreal feeling of impending death and return to the rhythm of work, although every time I moved, my step was tentative and my eyes cut to the trapdoor, despite an annoyed "I shut it" repeating inside my hood. I blasted the metal grating deck, then descended a few steps and, slapping the harness carabiner on the ladder, blasted under the crow's nest. Continuing working down the tower, two hours later I was all the way to the superstructure. Richards cut the pressure, letting me know it was time to knock off for lunch.

Climbing down, I removed my hood and stripped off my rain gear, tearing away the duct-taped cuffs. My side and back throbbed. Pulling up my shirt, an angry purple bruise circled half way round my waist.

I groaned and gazed out across Elliott Bay. Downtown Seattle looked like a Hollywood prop, a one-dimensional cutout framed against a solid blue background. That familiar scene always possessed the power to make me feel good, glad to be alive. Realizing the sentimental—now stupid and ironic—cliché, I chuckled, which made my side hurt worse. I walked toward the fantail and ran into Davis.

"So..." He looked at me, then his eyes shifted away. "You can knock out the rest of the sandblasting after lunch, right?" *Pure Davis.*

"I'm fine." Turning away from the foreman, I hollered over my shoulder, "I'll get it done," and walked the rest of the way to the fantail. Richards was stooped over the valves of the sand pot, and when he saw me, he stood up and reached for my shoulder. Richards was the guy who gave me a break and became my mentor, but this time I wasn't greeted with his usual smile. Richards's eyes narrowed and his tone was serious. "No more dancing up there, Nolan."

"No more dancing," I repeated, my words even and my features set. I was suddenly back in the principal's office.

He held my gaze for a moment, then his expression softened. Richards brought his face closer to mine and added in a low voice, "Seriously, you watch yourself, Nolan." His focus returned to the sand pot. "Ain't no job worth your life," he said without looking up, "you know what I mean?"

I jammed my hands into my coverall pockets and nodded in agreement, saying almost to myself, "I was on the razor's edge." The shrill shipyard whistle broke the tension. Richards and I walked the length of the main deck to the broad aluminum gangway and became part of the human current of a hundred workers leaving the ship for lunch.

After washing up in the locker room, I grabbed my lunch pail and sat down with the usual group of guys.

"Those Mariners are looking good in spring training," someone said. "Wait 'till the season starts, then they'll disappoint you," someone else replied. So none of the men at my table had witnessed my accident.

Taking a bite of sandwich, the banter became a monotone, and I drifted away. The world went sideways as I fell through the trapdoor again. Richards was right. . . that was the closest I'd come to dying. *There's nothing routine about this,* I told myself. *It requires experience and focus, and I lacked both today.* I mentally crossed off one of my nine lives and willed my attention back to the conversation.

The guys drained their coffee cups as the whistle blew, signaling the end of lunch. I stood slowly, once again sensitive to my side. I heard lunch pails being stashed and locker doors slamming. I took my time leaving, gingerly descending the creaky wooden staircase. Halfway down, my friend Lamar caught up to me. A light-skinned black man with almond-shaped eyes and a pencil-thin mustache, he put his hand on my shoulder, saying, "Yo, Master Blaster," in his singsong voice, "was that you up there, dangling from the crow's nest of the *Roark* this morning?"

Terrific. Lamar had seen me. I wasn't the master of anything at the moment, so I admitted, "Yeah, it was me," and looked away, continuing down the steps.

Lamar kept pace with me. "That's some pretty fancy sandblasting." His eyes danced as a cigarette bobbed up and down from his lips. "Kinda like in the circus."

I stopped. "Well . . . that's what sandblasters do," trying to sound cool about what happened.

Lamar knew better. "Yeah, right." His grin widened. "That and kill themselves." Lamar patted my shoulder as he walked down past me. "You take care up there, Brother Nols. We wanna keep you around." Then he turned back and laughed. "We gotta have us at least one white sandblaster in this shipyard, even if he really wants to be an ac-ro-bat."

Nodding and tipping my hard hat, I was smiling. "Right on, Lamar." Whatever the circumstances, he could get me into a good mood.

I walked across the yard in the direction of the *Roark*. Time to get back to work. *Maybe I can finish sandblasting this monster without killing myself in the process.*

The job was completed without any problems. Richards killed the pressure on the hose, and Davis showed up. "Okay, it looks like you got the blasting done," Davis said in his expressionless voice. "Here's your timecard." The whistle sounded as he abruptly turned and walked away.

No big deal; just another day of on-the-job training, sandblasting at Lockheed shipyard.

# THE SEQUIM CONNECTION

"The honey has quit running," my dad said. "Your mother and I have supported you through four years of college. Now it's time for you to go find a job—any job—and make something of yourself."

"You're right," I said, waving the white flag. "It's time for me to get out of here. Sequim can't do anything for me."

"Maybe it can, and maybe it can't, but you won't know until you go somewhere. You've got to see what else is out there." Dad put his hand on my shoulder. "If it all falls apart, you can always come back. We'll be here. You'll only be a ferry ride away."

"I'd like to be...I don't know." I couldn't put into words *I want to be an up-and-coming guy in the big city with a great job, making a pile of money.*

As if he could read my thoughts, my dad smiled. "Well, the first step in reaching *any* goal involves you finding work, right?"

Dad loaned me four hundred bucks to get started, along with the use of my mother's highly temperamental car. Armed with my bachelor's degree, I said "so long" and sped away on a crisp summer morning heading east to Seattle. I was twenty-three years old and, if not ready to conquer the world, at least hungry to experience a little more of it.

Familiar stands of Douglas fir streamed by my car, reflecting in the windshield, and the scenery began to work its accustomed magic on me. Upbeat by nature, my buoyant mood increased as I wound along the highway. My ears were filled with the song of the future calling me. My destination was my older sister's house, where I intended to take up residence and make the next big step in my life: a journey to find a job and to find myself.

My sister Nancy lived with her husband, Dave, in a modest bungalow in the Beacon Hill neighborhood, in the southeast part of the city. With two small kids at home, their tiny house was already crowded, so my visits always landed me in the living room on their lumpy green couch.

"Hey, little brother," she greeted me at the door, wrapping me in a genuinely warm bear hug. "I've got everything fixed up for you. This is going to be great." Nancy, always the mom, likely had a secondhand toothbrush set aside for me in the bathroom.

That afternoon I sat, coffee cup in hand, poring over the newspaper in Nancy's kitchen. It was the late seventies, disco music was sweeping the country, and finding a job began with scouring the Help Wanted section of the *Seattle Times*. The page was large and the newsprint was small, so by my rose-colored calculation, there were hundreds, maybe even thousands, of job openings waiting to be filled.

The search itself stoked the fires of my enthusiasm. I circled promising ads with a black felt-tipped marker, sometimes reading them out loud to Nancy, who looked up from her housework and responded with encouraging words like "Oh, sounds good" or "Yes, that job *is* promising" or "A perfect fit for you, Mike!" Her pregame pep talk built me up even more, if that was possible.

Reality hit hard the following morning when I tried to track down addresses in the city to fill out applications. I wasn't familiar with Seattle. I didn't know the layout of the downtown streets. I had a hard time finding a place to park. By the end of the first day, I'd turned in a grand total of four applications. "Looking for work," I admitted to my sister that evening, "is a full-time job in itself."

As the days went on, I continued filling out applications but didn't have any follow-up meetings or interviews. Over and over I heard nothing but "Thanks, we'll let you know."

What was I doing wrong? All applications included a space for "level of education," which I eagerly filled in, but there was never a question about what I'd learned or anywhere to brag, "I graduated with honors." The largest space on each application was "list previous employment history here," which I left blank. Although I had worked since I was fourteen, I didn't consider jobs like "dishwasher" and "short order cook" impressive enough to mention.

I was the get-along kid in the background who didn't push the issue or have the confidence to advertise myself. My laid-back approach worked well enough for me at college, where I knew who I was and what I was doing. For four years I'd stated with assurance, "I'm a biology major working on my bachelor's degree," which had a nice, self-comforting ring to it. Now that sense of identity was gone. I kept pursuing want ads and filling out applications through blind faith. What else was I supposed to do? I continued going through the newspaper, expecting something to happen. Looking back, my perspective was based on a lot of assumptions. All along I'd assumed that if I went to college, worked hard, and earned a degree, a well-paying job would magically fall into my lap. I never considered what needed to happen between earning that degree and being offered a job. What I knew was that I'd kept my nose to the grindstone at Gonzaga University, just as I was supposed to. College was worth it, right? My degree was going to help me, wasn't it? The applications kept going out, but the inescapable fact was that, in the Jimmy Carter years, the economy was floundering. I maintained a daily facade of optimism with my sister, but I was becoming disenchanted, feeling I wasn't prepared for anything, didn't know what I was doing or where I was going.

I continued filling out applications, and after three weeks I started exhausting the Help Wanted section of the newspaper. Was that even possible? I tried not to show it, but getting absolutely nowhere made me begin to crack. Everything was *not* okay. I started avoiding my sister. Phone calls to my dad became shorter and then disappeared altogether. An undercurrent of panic led me to leave the want ads behind and take to the streets. I developed the "Big Building Theory," which states that large downtown office buildings employ vast numbers of people, so by locating the personnel office in these buildings, I would encounter multiple job openings. If nothing else, I still possessed the logical thinking of a science major.

My scientific theory paid off, but not until I was brought face-to-face with the most humiliating encounter of my job search. There I was, deep within the bowels of a towering building—my third that day—sitting across the desk from a humorless middle-aged secretary. She peered at me through cat's- eye glasses, handing me an employment application as men and women in smart business suits hurried by, oblivious to my presence.

"List your educational background and qualifications here," she intoned in a flat voice while painted fingernails tapped annoyingly on the desktop, telegraphing she was offended by my asking for a job. It didn't take me long to fill out the application because my background and experience were so limited.

Handing back the paperwork, I tried to lighten things up by making a little conversation. "I recently graduated from college at—"

Holding my application in midair, she cut me off with an abrupt, "Where is *See-Que-Um?*" Her eyes shifted between me and the paperwork.

At that moment an athletic-looking man in a blue suit and horn-rimmed glasses walked by and, without stopping, said, "It's pronounced '*Skwim.*'"

"Whatever," the secretary said under her breath, looking back at me and dropping my application on her desk. "We are upgrading two keypunch operator positions. Do you have familiarity with computer languages?"

I'd studied Spanish in high school for two years but, beyond my mother tongue, that was the extent of my background in languages, computer or otherwise. I tried to formulate an intelligent response but hesitated as terms like Fortran and COBOL swirled through my head.

This was long before everyone in the world walked around with a computer in their back pocket. I recall the first time I *saw* a computer up close. It was 1974, and I was touring the Gonzaga campus as a new student. I was shown the "computer room" during the tour, because having one on campus was a big deal. The room was a glass-walled, temperature-controlled enclosure with an elevated floor. When I stepped inside, I heard a *swoosh* behind me as the opened door released a pressurized air seal. The space I walked into was antiseptic. Shiny gray rectangular metal boxes stood like oversized file cabinets, with switches and buttons and colored lights down the front. The cabinets blinked and hummed. Someone explained this hermetically sealed room was equipped to keep out "computer bugs." I thought they were referring to actual insects.

"No, I don't know Fortran or COBOL," I said, at least acknowledging the names of two computer languages in an effort to sound halfway intelligent.

The secretary's response was a derisive snort, translating into *Who is this moron, anyway?* "Well, are you familiar with Applesoft BASIC?"

*Did she say apple sauce?* "Ah...no..."

She stood up, exasperated, and leaned forward on her arms. Her voice went up a decibel as she stared directly at me. "Can you type?"

Again, I hesitated. I had been a science major, an honor student, and now I sat unarmed and naked. The truth was, in college I always managed to convince my girlfriend to type my term papers, so no, I'd never learned to type. "Well...no..."

"CAN YOU FILE?" She was practically yelling at me now.

My cheeks grew warm, and I cast my eyes down to my shoes, loathing myself and trying to compose my thoughts so I could say something in my defense. My mouth opened but words failed me. When I looked up, there was a smile of pure contempt on her face, and it dawned on me she was enjoying herself. Strike three. I shut my mouth and stood to find the door.

The man in horn-rimmed glasses passed by again, this time with a stack of papers under one arm. He stopped in front of me. "So, you're from Sequim?"

I cleared my throat and, without looking up, said, "That's where I went to high school."

"Sequim. Yes. Lovely place." He set the stack of papers on the desk. "My parents retired there."

As I looked up at him, I caught the secretary rolling her eyes. The man bent forward and picked up my application. "And you—ah, let's see—are Mr. Nolan." He adjusted his glasses, adding, "And...you're looking for a job with us."

"Yes, that's right." I straightened up and got my game face back on.

"Well," he said with an air of confidence, "I'm sure we can find something for you." He tucked the stack of papers back under his arm, still holding my application. "Please come with me, Mr. Nolan. We can meet in my office."

He marched down the hallway and I followed, head held high, hearing, "Sequim, yes, terrific place..." I set aside all of the wonderful things I had rehearsed about my college education, and said, "It's a *great* little town. So you've spent time there in Sequim?"

*Author Intro*

# CRAIG ANDREWS

My Muse is a poet, and so it seems am I. The two of us make a team. We fit together. We mutually inspire. I am never angry with my Muse. I trust Her completely and give Her free reign to explore. Together we inhabit a world a little less used than what most people know.

I love to write about what lays before me, but perhaps one-half into this other world; the lawn which needs to be mowed, the frog on the doorstep, but all with a heart spirit brimming and a twinkle in the eye.

Life, I feel, is a magical gift which I hope that I will never get used to. Being human is a difficult job and perhaps a little clumsy, but I try to be kind.

Craig can be reached at tarasparkman@yahoo.com

# THE SPRING LAWN

The grass will not wait,
It will not wait for the rain to stop,
It will not wait for a full week between mows,
It grows with the urgency of a starving being,
It wildly sings the arias of Spring,
It is in a constant orgasm of Maranatha

Why am I charged with this endless job of reeling
    it back in,
Of cutting it into compliance?
It is like a teenager on dope,
Basically out of control,
The neighbors slow down, look at our lawn as
    they drive by,
The peer pressure is intense,
They say that we do this because it reminds us
    of the open savannah of our birth
But the open savannah was not mowed,!?
I don't know
But I have to admit that the satisfaction of a
    freshly cut lawn does run deep,
Even if it is only for a day.

# CONTENTMENT

On a clear morning in late October
I put on my coat and stroll out into the garden,
Placing the chair just so
I settle in, close my eyes and feel the warmth of
    the sun cascade across my head, face, and body,
The cat curls up next to me,
The old dog wanders over and lays in the cozy
    gravel of the driveway,
The sounds of my wife quietly puttering with
    her tomatoes cradles my senses,
And I am lost,
Totally immersed into a deep pond of delight;

There is only Life,
It took eleven billion years to bring me to the
    place of this contented sigh,
I am no longer human,
I am only a vastness of gratitude.

# IT'S A WRAP!

Stretched out in nocturnal repose,
Cozy and warm in your arms,
We cracked open the window to let in the cool
    of the night and fall of the rain;

I know of  no greater wisdom than what I can
    hear on the roof and on the leaves,
Nor what greater love than the Nature of
    our Home.

# THE SWALLOW

The swallow spreads her wings
Eludes the hawk
And returns to her nest,
She is unconcerned,
I am concerned,
Lest she lay scattered,
A stain on the road which leads through these
    rocks,
And the hawk?
Hunger drives him
Back into the game of availability,
Of time, and death;

There is suffering,
All things partake of that cup,
But it is only the human who feels the edge
    of angst
Fearful of the loss
Unable to look into the eye of what is truly sweet,
And then let it return to naught.

## SHELDRAKE THE BLACKSNAKE

Sheldrake the Blacksnake went slithering towards the door
His heart beat fast
Lest the kitchen lass discover him on the floor,

Into the house he chased a mouse
Who laughed and got away,
Now he's told
For a step so bold
This could be his final day,

His sister Sue became a stew
In a house not far away,
"Oh why!"
"Oh why!"
Came his plaintive cry
Though Fate must have its say,

The day is sweet with waving grass
The sun is warm
He's close
He's fast,
When comes a shriek to wake the dead
And a cleaver aimed right at his head!

Using strength he never knew
The race was on
He fairly flew!
Through the door
And to the log
Between the toes of a collie dog

And to this day
He couldn't say
What Angel helped him get away,

But the tip of his tail
He left behind
A warning to all who would cross that line,
That the dwelling of Man
Is a perilous place
For all who would give the mouse a chase.

# THE ROAD TO WELLNESS

People send me "Get Well" cards which usually
    arrive after I am already well
And this makes me very superstitious,
But perhaps, "Well" is something which I am
    always aspiring to
Like a horse at full gallop just inches too far
    ahead for my lasso and I can't quite seem to
    close the gap,
Or, perhaps, Life is never "Well"
But always just becoming
And if you pursue the concept of "Wellness"
    you are, at least, pointed in the right direction?
I don't know,
My brain is a dangerous implement
Which I am not sure that I should be allowed
    to wield unnecessarily,
Feed me well
Love me for what I am,
I will try to be docile.

# HAMMER

Boy! You've sure been through it!
A loyal and brave guy
You've lived everywhere,
Seen it all,
Now you get some time off at Grandma's and
    Grandpaw's,
Lots of love and good things to eat;
You're a little broad in the beam
And your back legs barely work to get you
out to poop,
But when you're feeling good
And you go for a walk up the street
You become a BIG smile
Wearing a dog.

# THANKSGIVING

I am caught in a mind burp
Gazing out from my place at the table
Into the Field of Animation
The ups and downs and crisscross of things
    being passed
A whole new world of meaning shown by arms,
    hands, and fingers, gesticulating in fantastic ways
Language which is not the simple melody of
    one-on-one talk
But a whole orchestra of human speech blended
    together into something not disharmonious
I think that my fork must be half-way to my mouth
I have grunted answers to questions that I
    did not hear
I realize that I may be in danger
I grasp hold of the thigh of the person sitting
    next to me
I hope it is my wife.

# PLATFORM

I have danced in the rain until I was sopping wet
    and shivery cold,
I have sung arias with the wind which played
    the eves of my home like a flute of many holes,
Yesterday I must have carried a hundred stranded
    earth worms from the wet asphalt to the ground
    once again -
And one grateful newt who crawled onto my hand
    to be ferried across the road, escaping almost certain
    destruction;
The People of the Day are curled up in an angst
    of helplessness as they gaze into a world which
    makes no sense,
They cry out, "What can I do."
But I have made new friends of the rain and the wind,
And if there were a million of me then there would
    be a hundred million more worms to work their
    magic into the ground
And a million more grateful newts to make our
    world a friendlier place
"Work the Simple Virtues," I say,
Hold the Ground,
And above all,
Carry newts!

# CONSIDER THIS

What is truly wild is the Mind of the people,
It is the unexplored frontier
the realm beyond reason
The place which astounds,
And it is here,
From this place where our thoughts cannot follow
That our help shall surely come,
For just as Life itself
Flows from out of the place unseen
We are an aria of impossibilities,
We do not come from out of the loins of Gods
Nor the loins of each other,
But are birthed, moment by moment, from out
    of nothing at all,
We are lost in an enchantment of Now;

"Consider this," said a friend of mine, "that Now
    is a state of constant change, and never, even
    for an instant, is it ever found to be the same; yet
    it is always found in the same place, and like the
    still heart of an enchanted flower, Eternity
    dances upon its captured present."

# THE TWO FACES OF LIFE

She said, "I touched the Sun."
And that part of you which is the scientist says,
    "No, that is not something that you could do."
But that part of you which is the Mystic says,
    "What was it like?"

63512370R00186

Made in the USA
Middletown, DE
27 August 2019